I turned the last page and ~~...~~ *ring at the face of a young man . . . it was my face looking at me. A few years older, but my face. But it couldn't be!*

When Dominic finds the photograph in his grandad's loft, at first he can't believe what he is seeing. How can it be possible? How can there be someone else looking so like him? And then it begins to dawn on him that this must be his brother. But why has he never been told that he had a brother? Why has it been kept secret? And what happened to him?

When his parents refuse to tell him anything, Dominic decides to find out the truth for himself. But when he starts his search, Dominic uncovers a horrifying secret and unleashes a chain of events that will have far-reaching and disastrous consequences for everyone involved.

Alison Allen-Gray was brought up in the wilds of Suffolk. She gained a BA Hons in English and Drama at university in Wales and then co-founded a performing arts centre, converted from an old cinema, on the south coast of England. She has co-written two children's musicals and one for adults whilst also developing her acting career, mainly in children's theatre. Alison had her first picture book published in 1998 and still lives by the coast in Sussex. She enjoys fellwalking, horse riding, and going on long trips abroad with her partner in their vintage sports car. *Unique* is her first novel for Oxford University Press.

Unique

Other Oxford fiction

Unique

Alison Allen-Gray

OXFORD
UNIVERSITY PRESS

The author and publisher wish to make it
known that the contents and characters
of this book are purely fictional.

OXFORD

Great Clarendon Street, Oxford OX2 6DP

Oxford University Press is a department of the University of Oxford.
It furthers the University's objective of excellence in research, scholarship,
and education by publishing worldwide in

Oxford New York

Auckland Bangkok Buenos Aires
Cape Town Chennai Dar es Salaam Delhi Hong Kong Istanbul
Karachi Kolkata Kuala Lumpur Madrid Melbourne Mexico City Mumbai
Nairobi São Paulo Shanghai Taipei Tokyo Toronto

Oxford is a registered trade mark of Oxford University Press
in the UK and in certain other countries

Copyright © Alison Allen-Gray 2004

The moral rights of the author have been asserted

Database right Oxford University Press (maker)

First published 2004

All rights reserved. No part of this publication may be reproduced,
stored in a retrieval system, or transmitted, in any form or by any means,
without the prior permission in writing of Oxford University Press.
Within the UK, exceptions are allowed in respect of any fair
dealing for the purpose of research or private study, or criticism or
review, as permitted under the Copyright, Designs and Patents Act 1988,
or in the case of reprographic reproduction in accordance with
the terms of the licences issued by the Copyright Licensing Agency.
Enquiries concerning reproduction outside these terms and in other
countries should be sent to the Rights Department, Oxford University Press,
at the above address.

This book is sold subject to the condition that it shall not, by way of trade or
otherwise, be lent, re-sold, hired out or otherwise circulated without
the publisher's prior consent in any form of binding or cover other than that in
which it is published and without a similar condition including this condition
being imposed on the subsequent purchaser.

British Library Cataloguing in Publication Data available

ISBN 0 19 275335 5

1 3 5 7 9 10 8 6 4 2

Typeset by AFS Image Setters Ltd, Glasgow

Printed in Great Britain by
Cox & Wyman Ltd, Reading, Berkshire

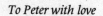

To Peter with love

PROLOGUE

I am high up in the mountains, sitting on their shoulders, breathing the rock-cold smell of sheep and earth and granite. Way down below me, where the dark slopes plunge towards each other, a pale mass is floating in the valley. A whipped-cream of mist. The sun is bleeding over the ridge opposite, but it hasn't got down into the valley yet. Somewhere down in that valley there are dead bodies. Dead because of me.

A crow squarks, sudden and close. It is time to begin the journey home.

1

On the day it all began, I'd spent a hot hour in the reception area outside my father's office. I reckoned he was keeping me waiting on purpose, leaving me to cook slowly in the midday sun that was burning through the glass. We were on the top floor of the tower, the penthouse suite, which was for his use only, and I'd been instructed to come here straight from school with my end of term report. It was the big one, the one that would indicate, he said, how well I should do in my exams next year.

I fidgeted on the leather sofa, turning the envelope over and over in my hands and wondering if it was possible to feel this sick without actually being sick. The receptionist looked up and smiled. She was a new one. They never stayed long. Lucky them. I wished I could change jobs, be someone else's son.

A buzzer went off and the sick feeling churned at my stomach.

'Mr Gordon will see you now, Dominic,' said the receptionist cheerfully, as if this was good news.

I pushed at the steel door. The huge chair behind his desk was empty. He was over by the window, looking down on his empire.

'Good afternoon, Dominic!'

'Hello, Dad,' I said.

He spun round to stare at me thoughtfully, savouring the cleverness which he always used as a weapon. People said he didn't look his age. He had his hair carefully dyed so as to have just the right amount of grey in the black. Contact lenses brightened the blue of his eyes and expensive dressing did the rest. He was a handsome man, people said. He would be sixty this year and any normal person who'd made as much money as he had would have retired long before then.

'Do you know, Dominic,' he said, with a puzzled frown, 'I've always had a strong belief that there is no problem that cannot be fixed. However, I am, as they say, damned if I can see how to fix this one.'

An alarm bell went off in my head. He must have already seen my report. He gestured to the creased, slightly damp envelope in my hand.

'Open it,' he said. 'Let us see if, by some miracle, your copy holds more hope for your future than does the one I've had emailed through.'

He strode over to his desk and jabbed at the keyboard of his communications centre. The screen snapped into life.

'I said open it.'

I ripped at the envelope. Surely, surely it couldn't be that bad. I'd worked really hard. I pulled out the little red book with its gilded school crest and flicked through with trembling fingers to look at the grades.

'Have you anything to say?' he asked.

'I'm sorry,' I said, crushed with misery. One C—that was for biology—the rest of the sciences were Ds. I didn't get as far as Art and English because my father took the book away.

'It makes interesting reading,' he said. 'Your chemistry master, for example, suggests that "Dominic needs to apply his brain". Upon further investigation, we find that this is a common theme. Dominic, when you take up a senior position in this company it must be seen that you do so on merit and not simply because you are my son. I do not want

4

the embarrassment of a son for whom I have to apologize the whole time! Such laxity is totally unacceptable!'

. . . Blah, blah, blah . . .

Now, as I lean back against my mountain, my stomach wrings with anger. He had said it. I was totally unacceptable and I always had been. But he'd never told me why. If I'd fought him back then, would it have made a difference?

Anyway, I didn't fight. On that baking summer afternoon I stared out of the window of the European headquarters of Gordon's Pharmaceuticals, and watched the monorails shuttling around the city. Tubes full of people. I knew that I didn't want to spend my life sitting in this tower. But I was too terrified to say what I did want— I don't think I even knew back then. Back then, only a couple of months ago.

'Clearly, these grades do not augur well for your university prospects,' he said. 'In view of the cost of your education . . . Dominic, are you listening to me?'

'Sorry.'

I'd been looking at the blocks of colour in the cityscape below. A tessellation of murky reds and greys. Was tessellation the right word, though? Did a tessellation have to be made up of all the same shapes? There were so many shapes down there . . .

'You do propose to try for Oxford or Cambridge, I take it?' my father said. 'Cambridge, preferably.'

'I hadn't . . . I don't know,' I mumbled, avoiding his eyes. Despite the swimming-pool blue, they were like a hawk's eyes. And I was the mouse. Pinned down while he ripped at me.

'Or do you intend to spend the rest of your life grubbing around your grandfather's house and painting pictures?'

My heart thudded. How did he know I did my painting at Pops's place? I gasped in the breath to make a protest but stopped myself. Best to keep my mouth shut where Pops was concerned. I didn't want my father laying down laws that I would have to break. And I certainly didn't want him turning up at Pops's place.

'I'll try and do better, I promise,' I said.

Pops needed me and I needed Pops. There was a thing he used to say to me when I was little: 'I'd kill a dragon for you.' And I'd kill a dragon for him, too.

'Oh, you *will* do better, Dominic, rest assured you will. At this point, however, an explanation would be most acceptable.'

'I'm really sorry, Dad. I *did* try, honest. I just can't . . . ' I stopped, remembering that 'can't' wasn't in his vocabulary.

My father had finished an orbit of the office and was coming in to dock at the desk.

'I'll be flying out shortly and will be away on business for a few days,' he said. 'By the time I return, you will have a tutor to get you up to speed on your sciences over the summer holiday. As I say, there's no problem that can't be fixed. You may go. The chauffeur will take you home.'

He turned back to his communications centre and switched off the screen.

So that was the summer blown.

And just my luck, the chauffeur waiting for me wasn't the nice guy who could be persuaded to release you at an unauthorized destination. It was Granite-face. No chance of getting him to drop me off at Pops's house. I'd have to go home first.

The car purred up to the iron security gates of our mansion and Granite-face scanned his pass. The gates swung slowly open. The mansion was a new one, an Exclusive Executive Home, sitting smug and sun-drenched within its high walls. I often wondered what, exactly, 'exclusive' meant. Exclusive of life, I reckoned. No birds or insects. No worms burrowing in the lawns, no bees flitting from flower to flower. Nothing that would muck up the gleaming tidiness.

I chucked a few yells around the house and across the shaved lawns to see if Mum was around. She wasn't, but I found a note by the phone: 'The cat has been sick on your bed, so be careful. Back later. Love you, love you, love you. Mum.'

I closed the door on the silent house and set off on the walk to Pops.

2

I tried very hard not to let the outside world know just how far gone Pops was, because I knew it would kill him if the authorities got involved and tried to put him into a Retirement Unit. Truth is, he's woofing mad, but between the two of us that never matters.

On that afternoon, as usual, I rang the bell and waited. You can't hear the doorbell from outside, so you never know if it's worked or not until the door suddenly opens and there he is.

There he was, that afternoon, with a face like a burst football. Which meant that the false teeth had gone missing again. Eventually, I found them in the fruit bowl. He took the teeth and turned away from me like an impressionist donning a new disguise.

'Dear boy!' He swung round to greet me. 'Just a short back and sides will do. Where do you want me?'

So, that day I was to be a barber.

I plonked a chair in front of the dining-room mirror, got the comb from his dressing-table and the scissors from the kitchen.

He smiled at me in the mirror.

'Got to make the effort, haven't you? Even at my age. Keep yourself nice.'

'You always look nice.'

'Good, good. Make sure my daughter pays you. She looks after all that sort of thing. Takes care of me.'

You must be joking, I thought. Mum doesn't take care of anyone. But, of course, he wasn't joking. I drew the comb through his fragile silver hairs and wondered whether she would be sober when she got back from wherever it was she'd gone. I thought about her note and smiled to myself. 'The cat has been sick on your bed, so be careful.' Careful of what?

I caught Pops's glance in the mirror.

'Sweet girl, my daughter,' he said. 'Sings like an angel, did you know? Shouldn't boast of it, but, you know, a chap has a right to be proud of his little girl! Singing at the Opera House next week!'

'That's brilliant!'

I carried on combing. I knew this story about Mum the rising opera star and her leading role at the Opera. For Pops, the story ended there, with a standing ovation and roses thrown onto the stage. He had forgotten the bit where her career stopped dead because suddenly she couldn't sing any more. Nobody had ever told me why. They hadn't wanted to talk about it.

'Did I tell you, my daughter sings like an angel?' He smiled.

'You did mention it once,' I said casually. 'What sort of stuff does she sing?'

'Very, very talented.' He nodded.

I stroked my hand over the tea-coloured blotches on his nearly bald head. Most of the things that had gone in there over eighty-two years were lost somewhere in the grey folds and ripples of the brain. Some memories found their way back every now and again. Like the day he told me, in precise detail, how to take off and land a light aircraft.

Suddenly he leapt up, hair half-chopped, with a long wisp of grey sticking straight up on top of his head.

'Better start packing!' he cried. 'Should have thought of it sooner!'

And he was off down the hallway at full speed.

'Where are you going?' I called after him.

9

'Awful lot to do before we go! Come along, Dominic!'

I followed him up the dusty stairs to the landing, where he stopped suddenly and wagged a finger up at the ceiling. I looked at the trapdoor. I'd only ever half-noticed it before.

'You want to get into the attic?' I said.

'Got to get the cases down!' he cried.

'Is there a ladder?'

'There's a stick,' he said. 'You do it with a stick.'

Soon, behind one of the bedroom doors, I found the stick. It had a hook on the end and I hooked it round a ring on the trapdoor and pulled. Down came a folding ladder.

'Ah-HA!' cried Pops.

You know you're in for trouble when he says 'Ah-HA!'

I held the ladder steady while he climbed up. He found a light switch and by the time I got up there he was standing in a pool of light like an actor on a dusty stage.

He grinned at me. Then frowned, and said, 'What the hell are we doing up here?'

'Packing?' I suggested.

'Yes. Yes, you're quite right,' he said.

And then he was off again, hopping across the attic like an old mountain goat.

'Look at this! Remember this?'

He dragged a moth-eaten cover from a table. On the table was a racetrack with old toy cars scattered around it. He picked up one of the cars and fixed it on the track.

'Used to play this with my grandson!' he cried.

'Did you?' News to me. I'd never seen the thing in my life before.

'Yes, yes! But you have to plug it in!' He found the plug and dangled it at me hopefully.

The hunt for a socket to stick the plug in involved Pops standing in the centre of the attic, directing me from one spidery corner to another.

'Must be one somewhere!' he cried.

'Ouch!' I cracked my head on a beam.

'Careful as you go! Nothing there? Goodness, my old brain needs a bit of a shake!'

He shook his head. It didn't seem to help.

At last I saw a socket behind a bulging tea chest. I tugged at the chest and it shifted on the gritty floor. It was full of heavy old books. I gave one more heave and the thing split open, books slapping out of it in clouds of dust.

I fell backwards.

'You all right, old chap?' said Pops.

'Yeah,' I spluttered as I plugged the thing in. It would probably blow us up, I thought, but what the hell.

I switched it on and a few seconds later there was the high-pitched whine of little electric cars whizzing round the track. Pops was standing over the table, squeezing the control buttons, eyes and mouth wide. I began to stack the books back into what was left of the tea chest. And then I noticed that not all of them were books. There were a couple of musty albums with old-fashioned photos.

'BAH!' cried Pops. I dropped the album I had in my hand.

'What is it?'

He didn't answer, too absorbed with picking up a fallen car and fitting it back onto the track. The whining noise started again.

I opened the album. The story began with Pops and Gran and a baby. This must be Mum. Even as a bald, pink-faced bundle in Gran's arms she had a faint trace of the dimples that she and I both have. Silently, I flicked through the pages and watched her grow. Sandcastles and sports days, rain-soaked camping holidays, dogs, cats, and birthdays. Pops and Mum hugged together, Mum holding some sort of trophy. I imagined myself into the pictures, trying to feel

11

what a happy family would have been like. I bet the birthday cake had been made by Gran herself, she looking on proudly as my five-year-old mother blew out her candles. I wanted more of this perfect childhood. I picked up the next album.

But here was Mum grown up, and now she had a baby. Me!

The first picture was just us—Mum looking ages younger than she did now, her long dark hair framing my bald head as she snuggled me against her cheek. Then there was Dad holding me. It was obviously Dad because it was his face, but the face was wearing an expression that I couldn't remember seeing lately, if ever. He was smiling. In fact he looked happy. So there must have been a time when I'd done something to please him.

I flicked him over and saw myself as a chubby baby sitting in the bath, chewing a plastic duck. Opposite, I was smiling straight to camera, looking tottery, with Mum holding my arms while I walked. Next, me and Mum and Gran, and then a nursery school line-up. I searched along the rows and found myself wearing (yuck!) a stupid cheesy grin, dimples the same as Mum's. Come to think of it, I still had that stupid cheesy grin!

I searched on hungrily, annoyed that they'd never shown me these bits of the past that belonged to me. All I'd ever seen were the cringe-making DVDs that we didn't bother to look at any more.

There was me playing with Pops in a tree house. I stared at the photo. How old was I? About five? I couldn't remember Pops coming out to visit us in the States, but perhaps Mum and Dad had brought me over here.

'Pops?' I said. 'Do you remember going to visit us in the States and playing with me in a tree house—when I was little?'

'Tree house? What d'you want to live in a tree for?'

12

'Never mind.'

I flicked on through and watched myself getting older. Me on a tiny bicycle and then . . . something that puzzled me. Me in a school uniform, when I was about eight. But what was I doing wearing a uniform? They didn't have uniforms in the States. I stared into the picture. I was with Dad, holding his hand. We were on the steps of what looked like an English stately home. They often tried to make things look English in the States. It could have been a school or some wealthy person's house. Either way, I didn't remember the place.

I carried on turning pages. I began to panic. There were scenes with other kids that looked as if we were the best of friends, but I didn't remember them. Holidays I'd never had, places I'd never been. Yet there I was, right in the middle of it all, living a life I didn't remember. And the really weird thing was that Mum and Dad looked somehow different from the way they did in my memory of the DVDs that I used to play. But *how* they were different I couldn't quite tell. There was a light-heartedness about them. And something else.

I turned the last page and felt myself go hot all over. I was staring at the face of a young man. He was leaning against the parapet of an old stone bridge, his fair hair bright in the sunshine. There was a river, old buildings. It was my face looking at me. A few years older, but my face. But it couldn't be!

'Pops!' I stumbled towards him on wobbly legs and slid the album onto the table. 'Pops, who is this?'

He glanced down and I caught his eyes as slowly, slowly, he looked up again. Please come back and tell me, Pops, I willed him. Stop being mad, just for a second, and remember properly. Remember this.

And then I turned cold all over, because I could see he did remember something, and for a moment I saw the eyes

13

of my grandfather as they used to be. Clear, intelligent.
And frightened.

'Who is it, Pops?'

He began to shake.

'It's Dominic.'

I looked at the photo again.

'No, Pops, it can't be! *I'm* Dominic. This isn't me!'

3

He turned away from me.

'Pops? Did you hear me? It can't be Dominic!'

I moved round, grabbed his arm, tried to make him look at me. His eyes had glassed-over with tears.

'It can't be me. I don't remember any of this!' I tried not to shout. '*Please* tell me who it really is!'

'Ummm, well now . . . ' He shook his right hand by his side, as he always does when he's upset. 'Should offer you a drink before you go. My wife will ummm . . . my wife . . . '

I couldn't have felt worse if I'd punched him in the gut. It had been years since he'd mentioned Gran as though she were still alive. He began to sob.

I closed the album.

'Tell you what,' I said, trying to sound bright even though my own voice was shaking, 'let's go back down and see what's on the radio. I think there's that programme you like, about gardening.'

He brushed his sleeve across his eyes. 'Do I like gardening?'

'Yeah, it's your favourite thing.'

'Then I'd better not miss out, had I?' he said.

I went ahead of him down the ladder, guiding the threadbare slippers from rung to rung. He made a fuss about putting the ladder away and shutting the trapdoor but eventually I settled him in his chair with one of the audio tapes I had recorded to soothe him when he got upset—the gardening programmes were favourite.

15

'Woolly aphid is one of nature's most tiresome pests,' said the presenter.

'Quite right,' nodded Pops. 'How right you are!'

In the kitchen, my thoughts churned as I brewed the tea. How could I have had two lives—one I remembered and one I didn't—going on at the same time? It just wasn't possible.

I heard the front door and the 'Woooo-hoooo!' of Pops's neighbour, Margi, arriving.

'Fwoof!' she cried, grinning from the kitchen doorway. 'Hot or what? How is your grandfather today? Look, there's a cake here. I've been baking all day because Tom's brother's coming down and he doesn't half get through cake. Doesn't touch the sides. And here's some steak and kidney pie and washing powder. I'll do some vegetables . . .'

She clattered around the kitchen, easily finding the pans and plates she needed. I stared at the neatly-iced cake that she'd left on the table.

'Margi,' I blurted, 'who did you say the cake was for?'

'That one's for your grandfather, love. But he won't mind you having a chunk.'

'No, I mean . . . ' Brother. She'd said 'Tom's brother'. 'Margi,' I said, 'did you know Mum and my father before I was born?'

'No, my love, first time I met them was when you all came back from the States—five, six years ago it must be now.' She came over and stroked my cheek with her palm. 'Why? What's up, love?'

The kindness stung like acid. I swallowed hard.

'Nothing. Pops has got his gardening programme and the tea's just brewing. See you later, Margi. Thanks.'

It was a brother. No other explanation. It couldn't be me in those photos, so it had to be a brother. I wandered home, searching for clues in my life, anything that could point to his existence. There was nothing. I couldn't remember him for myself, and certainly no one else had ever mentioned him. Why not? And where was he now?

I let myself in the back door, made straight for the fridge and gulped down a pint of juice. The house still felt deserted. The smell of rotting vegetation from the dishwasher was simmering in the afternoon heat and suddenly I felt as if I was in someone else's house. The brother had changed who my parents were. He'd changed who I was.

'Hello, darling!'

I spun round and was immediately wrapped in Mum's hug. Something banged against my back and as she pulled away I saw it was a half-empty wine bottle. In her other hand was an empty glass.

She plonked the bottle down, swiped a hand through her dyed auburn hair and beamed at me. I hoped it was only the first bottle of the evening. Things were going to be difficult enough as it was.

4

'How did it go?' she asked. 'He wasn't too rough on you, was he?'

It was only the first bottle, you could tell. Nothing had started to blur in her eyes or her voice yet.

'Who?'

'Your father, of course! Oh, Dominic, you did keep the appointment to see him? There'll be hell to pay if . . .'

'Yes, yes, I saw him. My report wasn't good enough. No surprises there.'

Sadness washed over her face. I suppose she was hoping that this time one of us might get it right and end the war. I'd turn out to be Einstein or my father would morph into a kindly, wise, and tolerant being.

'I didn't get to see my Art grades,' I said, 'but they should be OK.'

She smiled and I noticed again the dimples that I had seen in all the happy pictures in the album. 'Of course they will be!'

She glugged more wine into her glass and grabbed my hand. 'Come into the garden and tell me all about it. We've got three days to ourselves while he's in Paris.'

I just couldn't figure out how Mum could have had another son and never mention it. My mum is one of those leaky people who can't hold things in.

Suddenly I found that she was looking at me, searching for something.

'Dom, are you all right?' she said.

And then I became leaky myself. Couldn't stop it.

18

'Mum, did I ever have a brother?'

Her face changed. It changed so much that I lost her. I couldn't find her in her own face. I'd never seen anyone look so frightened.

At last she whispered, 'How did you find out?'

My stomach turned. This wasn't the answer I'd wanted. I'd wanted her to say that there was no brother. To tell me something that would explain it all away and leave me an only child again. Something in her eyes—the terror, pain, whatever it was, gave me a clue.

'Is my brother dead?' I said.

I was still staring into the face of a stranger. I panicked.

'Mum! It's an easy question! Either he's dead or he isn't!'

She looked at me as if I'd hit her. The answer took ages to come.

'Yes, he's dead. He died at university, in Cambridge.'

'But why didn't you tell me about him?' I cried.

'I couldn't.'

She gulped down the last half of her glass.

'Why not?'

'Dom, it was just too painful, it was better left, it was a long time ago, before you were even born . . . '

'And you named me after him!'

She turned on me, tears glittering.

'*How did you find out his name?*'

'Pops told . . . '

'WHAT? You've been upsetting Pops?'

'I wasn't . . . !'

'You must never, EVER do it again! Just keep out of it!'

'But I've got a right to know!'

'You HAVEN'T! Children don't need to know everything! There are some things . . . '

She stopped because she saw that I was crying.

19

'Dom! I'm sorry. It makes no difference to how we feel about you . . . I'm sorry!'

Too late. I ran across the lawn, up the stairs, and locked myself into my room.

After a while, she tapped on the door, wanting to be forgiven. I ignored her and she went away. I lay thinking as the heat slipped out of the day. She was crashing about in the kitchen, and then music went on full blast. She'd be well into the booze by now.

I picked up my phone, wondering whether to call Steve or Pogo. I pressed the key for Pogo and immediately cancelled it. I'd only have to do the post-mortem bit on the exam results and his would be better than mine, so would Steve's. They were all clever at my school. That's what the school was all about.

In the end, I decided to try Indy, my mate from the States. I hadn't seen him since we left there six years ago, but we'd kept in touch. I pressed his number and heard the engaged tone. Just like Indy. He spent most of his waking hours talking.

Anyway, perhaps it would be easier to email. If you write it down you can stop when you want to, but with talking it isn't so easy.

I switched on my computer and began:

Hi, Indy

How you doing? I need to run something by you. How about an online chat? It's pretty urgent. Get back to me asap?

I looked at the words. How, exactly, did I expect Indy to help? Indy, who had great parents, great friends, no worries, was allowed to get on and do what he was good at, which was sport. The great thing about Indy was that life was a laugh and he always believed everything would turn out all right. But I had a feeling burrowing into my mind that this wouldn't turn out all right. You don't keep such a big thing secret for no reason.

I sent the message anyway and moments later my phone rang. I pressed the green button and a voice said, 'Hiya, Buddy! Pretty urgent, huh? Don't keep me in suspense!'

I laughed. 'Indy! I didn't think I'd get you!'

'You got me. What's the problem?'

'Well, it's difficult . . .'

'You gotta make it quick, though. You know Emma?'

Emma was a girl he'd been droning on about for months.

'Yeah, you've mentioned her once or twice,' I said.

'Got a date tonight. So what the hell am I gonna wear? And aftershave or not, d'you reckon?'

'You don't shave.'

'So? Jeez, some help you are! Anyhow, what's up with you?'

'Family stuff.' I tried to sound light-hearted about it. 'Indy, I need you to find out if my parents have ever said anything to yours about having another son.'

'Jeez! They're having a kid? At their age?'

'No, of course not! No, listen—they had a son before I was born. My brother. And I've just found out that he died. Only they never told me about him.'

'Why not?'

'Exactly. Why wouldn't they?'

'You serious? You got a secret brother?'

'No, Indy, I'm just making it up.'

'So—what kinda brother? How old was he when he . . . you know . . . left the pitch?'

'Older than me. About twenty, I suppose. He was at university.'

'How 'bout you just sit your folks down and ask 'em about the guy? Tell 'em you gotta right to know.'

'Indy, my parents aren't like yours. Mum's really upset that I've found out and Dad doesn't know yet but . . . I just don't know how he'll react.'

For the first time ever, I found myself listening to the sound of Indy lost for words. At last he let out a long breath and said, 'Maybe it's somethin' real bad. Maybe he killed himself—you know, drugs or somethin'.'

I hadn't thought of that. I turned the horror of it over in my mind as Indy went on cheerfully, 'Or maybe it was homicide. He was hacked to bits and dumped in the garbage . . .'

'Yeah, all right, Indy, thanks . . .'

'How 'bout you do a search on the Net?'

'Of course! Why didn't I think of that?'

'Can't be smart *and* good-lookin'. Unless, of course, your name's Indy Halliday. Hey, I gotta go. You call me, let me know what's happ'nin'.'

'I will. Good luck with Emma!'

'Like I need it! See ya!'

'Bye!'

I turned back to the computer and gazed at the bright screen. 'Children don't need to know everything,' Mum had said. But I wasn't a child and I needed to know this. Even if it was something really bad.

A sudden surge of music—one of Mum's opera pieces—swelled and died downstairs. There'd be no talking to her now. I chose a search engine, and typed in the name:

DOMINIC GORDON

5

Alist appeared and I gasped out loud at the very first item.

'Dominic Gordon. Deceased.'

I raced through it. It wasn't him. This guy had had the same name as us way back in the eighteenth century. He'd written a book about bone surgery.

There were pages and pages of Dominic Gordons. The only other thing I had to go on was Cambridge, so I refined the search with that and it seemed there had been loads of us studying at Cambridge too, including the bone surgeon. I'd have to refine it on date. I flopped back in my chair, cranking my brain up to do the mental arithmetic. Mum was born in 1957. Supposing my brother had been born when Mum was twenty, in 1977. He could have been at Cambridge from 1995. And Mum had said he'd died before I was born. I banged in the dates 1995–2001, clicked on GO, and this time only one Dominic Gordon appeared. My heart started hammering.

His dates were 1980–2001. This could be him.

Under his name was a list that I couldn't make sense of at first. It seemed to be a list of book titles, with dates ranging from 1999–2001. But then I saw that they weren't books, but essay titles, because the first two had won essay prizes. Then it said that he'd got a First Class for a dissertation. At the end, in bold, it said that he'd won the Professor Holt Prize for Outstanding Undergraduate work in Life Sciences.

Life Sciences! I scrolled down, wanting more, but the

next item was a picture. I began to shake as the fair hair appeared, the forehead. It was going to be that face again, that face from the album. The eyes appeared. I stared back and then, suddenly, a warning message snapped onto the screen, covering his half-grown face. Seconds later, the screen snapped to blue.

'Damn!' I thumped at the desk. 'NO!'

I raced the cursor around the screen, clicking on everything and anything but it was no good. Anyhow, my hand was shaking so much I had to let go of the mouse. Those eyes had been unmistakable—the same eyes as the face in the album, the same eyes I could see any time I looked in a mirror, the same fair hair. Unmistakably my brother. And he had been clever. Really, really clever at the one thing my father wanted me to be clever at. Science.

I switched the computer off and on again, stabbing viciously at the keyboard, but it wouldn't connect to the Internet. This had happened a lot recently. Sometimes you could get back in, sometimes you couldn't and you had to wait until the computer decided to co-operate. I'd been promised a whole new set-up if my exam results were good. Some hope of that now.

I tried again three times, tears of anger coming as I realized the thing just wouldn't work. I *had* to know how he'd died!

I sat back again, trying to calm my thoughts, and then I had an idea. I'd use my father's laptop! I leapt up, opened my bedroom door, and listened. The music downstairs had quietened and I couldn't hear Mum. Carefully, I moved along the landing to my father's study door and looked in. The moment my eyes took in the empty surface of the huge oak desk, I realized that he'd taken the laptop with him to Paris. Damn him!

I'd just stepped back onto the landing when I heard Mum's voice below me.

24

'Michael Gordon, please. What d'you mean "who's speaking"? It's his wife—not that it's any of your damned business. Just put me through!'

I swung back into my father's study, picked up his phone, and heard Mum crying, 'Michael? Michael, *please* be there, please answer the phone!'

And then my father's bullish voice.

'Carla? For God's sake, you do realize the time . . . '

'Michael, it's serious. It's about Dominic. You'll have to come home. I can't cope . . . '

'Give me strength!' said my father. 'What's wrong with the wretched child now? It's not drugs? Is that what's rotting his brain?'

'He's found out about his brother!' she sobbed.

My mother's sobbing, my father's icy silence. Between them they held a secret history. I waited.

At last my father's voice, thinner than before.

'What exactly has he found out?'

'That he had an older brother!' she shrieked.

'Don't get hysterical, Carla! He had an older brother, that's all!'

'That's ALL?' screamed Mum. 'He's MY CHILD! We've hurt him!'

She sobbed and screamed, calling him by every word she's ever told me not to use. Dad was shouting down the phone.

'For God's sake, calm down, Carla! I'll get the first plane back in the morning. I should be with you around nine. Just go to bed. Do nothing, say nothing. Carla! Can you hear me?'

I wanted to yell down the phone to him myself, but I didn't have the nerve. And then a crash from the hall made me slam down the receiver and bolt downstairs.

The telephone table was slewed across the parquet floor and Mum was lying, groaning, beside a smashed

25

lamp. The light from the kitchen was glinting on a pool of red.

'MUM!'

Even as I threw myself down beside her, I realized that it wasn't blood. A bottle of wine had spilled across the floor. But as I propped her up against the stairs I saw that she had cut herself. Little red beads were growing from a glistening line of blood on her forehead, joining together to trickle towards one eye.

Her groans followed me into the kitchen as I went to get the first aid kit.

'What have I done? Oh God, what have I done?'

'You've had a row with me, drunk a vat of wine, had a row with my father, and fallen over and whacked your head.'

'Oh.' She gave me a wobbly smile. 'So I'm not having a very good day.'

'Not really.'

She squinted at the first aid kit. 'What've you got in your little bed rox?'

'Insect repellent,' I said, 'an arm sling . . . '

'Have I cut my head?'

'Yes. Shut up and let me see. Why do first aid kits always have millions of corn plasters? Corns aren't an emergency, are they?'

'I love you so much. I'd do anything in the world for you!' she said.

'Try giving up drink,' I muttered. I don't think she heard me.

I cleaned the cut and patched it with some sticky things that made her look as if she'd got Frankenstein Monster stitches. There was no way I could get her up the stairs, so I made up the sofa bed in the lounge and poured her into it. As I was trying to take off her necklaces she grabbed my hand and wouldn't let go.

So I lay down beside her and eventually we both fell asleep.

Much later, something woke me up. There was a pale grey light outside and I could just make out the shape of Mum, sitting bolt upright, her head turned towards me.

'Dominic, is it you?' she whispered.

'Of course it's me.'

And she lay back, closed her eyes, and slept again. But I didn't sleep. I was wide awake as daylight broke over us. I was making my plans.

6

My plans didn't include hanging around to wait for my father to arrive. While Mum was still sleeping, I wrote her a note saying I would be away for a few days and not to worry. Then I packed a rucksack and left the house.

First stop was the hypermarket. I couldn't do what I needed to do without money, so I had to know if my Junior ID card was still linked up to my father's account. If it was, he could pay for everything. It would be the first time in my life that I'd called the shots.

I got a trolley and whizzed up and down the deserted aisles, picking out all Pops's favourite things. Chocolate doughnuts, stuffed olives, roll-mop herrings, cullen skink, and Spam. I was on my way back to the checkout when I happened to glance down to the end of the warehouse and remembered that they had a computer section there. Maybe, just maybe, they sold laptops.

I headed back down the aisle and found a couple of laptops on display. Not very high spec, but then I didn't need all the lights and bells, I just needed Internet access. I quickly read the boxes and chose one, then ran, pushing the trolley up to speed and riding on it the last few yards up to the checkout. The checkout operative yawned and smiled.

'Early bird,' she said.

I grinned and unpacked my haul, watching as the things travelled along the conveyor belt. As the roll-mops were bleeped through, and then the laptop, I started patting my pockets.

28

'Oh *no*!' I cried, with what I hoped was a convincing wail of panic. 'Forgotten my money!'

The operative glared.

'Don't do this to me. If you've forgotten your Jiddy Card as well, we've both got a big headache!'

'Jiddy Card?' I said, innocently.

'Your Junior Identification, the kiddy card,' she said. 'It's against the law to be without it. It gives us access to a nominated account if you can't pay.'

'Oh, *yes*, I've got one of *those*, obviously,' I said.

I handed her my card. I'd never tried to use it for this before. I watched as she scanned it. She frowned, stabbed at a button on the scanner, then said, 'Right then, to be charged to the account of Mr Michael Gordon. I'll just ring through and get clearance.'

'Clearance? What for?' I cried.

'The credit limit's only £500. I have to ring Mr Gordon's bank before I can charge this amount to the card.'

'Oh. No, look, don't bother. Forget about the laptop, I'll come back another time. Will you just charge the food, please?'

My face was burning red. She hesitated, looking at me closely. If she thought I'd stolen the card and she called security, I was done for. I forced a smile.

'My dad said I could have a new one, but I guess he'd want to help me choose it himself,' I said.

She sighed and deducted the laptop from the total.

'OK, food only. Charged to the account of Mr Michael Gordon.'

'Thanks,' I muttered as I stuffed the food into bags. 'Have a nice day!'

On the way to Pops I stopped off at a cash point and got £200 out on the Jiddy. I didn't know how long I'd be away and I'd need cash for food and now also for an Internet café.

At last, I staggered into Pops's kitchen with the plastic carriers cutting into my hands.

'I've brought all your favourite things,' I puffed.

'Have you, dear boy? Extremely kind. Join me in a cocktail? Just having one myself.' He pointed to his mug of cold tea.

'I'll make us some more,' I said, filling the kettle. 'Look, Pops, I have to go away. Only for a day or so, though.'

'Aha!' he nodded.

'But Margi will come and do your tea as usual.'

'Aha!'

'And you can get Mum by pressing number one on the phone. I've put a red sticker on it, remember?'

'Are those chocolate doughnuts?'

'Yes, help yourself.'

I felt mean, diverting his attention with doughnuts while I sneaked off to the attic. I'd left the photo album on the racetrack table and I needed that photo of him—my brother. It would only take me a couple of minutes to get it.

I creaked up the last few rungs of the ladder, scrabbled around, hit the light switch and stood blinking in the light. I glanced across to the table. The album wasn't there.

Impossible! I went to check.

Gone.

Only Pops could have moved it.

He hadn't put it back in the tea chest. I searched in boxes, drawers, and trunks. He hadn't put it anywhere that I could find. I went back to the table and stared down at the racetrack, this strange, old-fashioned game that my brother had once played. My eyes suddenly stung with tears. I needed to know who my brother was. But Pops didn't want me to know. Mad as he was, not knowing who his family were or what day of the week it was, he did know that he didn't want me to have that album. They were all ganging up to stop me knowing anything.

I picked up the control for one of the cars. It fitted so neatly into my hand. I squeezed it till my hand hurt and then smashed it down on the table.

I clattered down the ladder and stood trembling on the landing. It was wrong to be angry with Pops, I knew that. But I was frightened.

Well, it just showed that I was right to do what I was going to do. Nobody else was going to help me, so I'd have to help myself.

I put the ladder away and went downstairs. I settled Pops in the lounge with his doughnuts and tea.

And then I headed towards the railway station to buy my ticket to Cambridge.

7

'Will you be requiring breakfast on the train?' asked the man at ticket sales.

Yes, I would be requiring breakfast. I would be requiring anything I liked so long as my father was paying. I bought a ticket with executive breakfast and sundry beverages.

I love trains. This one was a huge, gleaming, silver-and-black eel of a train, capable of nearly 300km per hour. The sun's warmth was beginning to seep through the great glass canopy of the station and people were swarming towards the train with trolleys and suitcases. I found a carriage near the nose and swiped my ticket. The door hissed open.

I sank into a window seat with a table and watched the last few people on the platform. Please, please don't let there be anyone who knows me, I thought. With a rush of panic, I remembered the Truant Patrols. But no, it was Friday and we always reckoned they bunked off on a Friday. And then I remembered something else. School had broken up. So no Truant Patrols anyway. I leaned back on the seat. I must try and relax, try to think straight and not look like someone who's on the run. I spread my things out on the seat and waited. My stomach was fluttering. Surely it was time to go? A bullet train was never late departing. But even as I looked at the platform clock, one of the great pillars holding up the canopy began to slide across its face. We were slipping noiselessly out into the hot morning.

Once we were under way, I began to get really excited.

Even the executive breakfast was an adventure. As I bounced my fork off the little pile of white rubber on my plate, the old lady opposite leaned forward: 'I think it's scrambled egg, dear, but I wouldn't swear to it.'

We laughed.

After breakfast, I stared out of the window and began to create my brother as I wanted him to be. The two of us together, plus a mum who didn't get drunk and a proper dad who helped you with things instead of putting you down all the time. No, leave them out of it. Too hard to imagine them changing. Just my brother and me. We'd be best mates. He'd be someone I'd turn to when things got on top of me. He'd never make me feel small. I could talk to him about art and stuff, and he could talk to me about . . . science. My thoughts plummeted back to ground like a shot bird as I remembered all those prizes he'd won. He'd be the clever one, the one who could do what Dad wanted and be good at scientific things, just like Dad was.

He must have been pretty brilliant to get to Cambridge University in the first place. Suddenly my father's words came back to me—what he'd said, only yesterday, about me trying for Oxford or Cambridge—'Cambridge preferably'. Preferably I should be like my brother. And what would my brother think of me if he knew me? Would he be just the same as my father? Would he think I was stupid?

Feelings swirled like colours in my mind. I'd always invented companions for myself. Perfect companions. If you get fed up with them, kick them out and invent a new one. But a real brother who'd lived a real life with my parents . . . Had they loved him more than me? The truth drenched through me. It all made sense now. My father's bullying, Mum's drinking. Perhaps even Pops going mad. I was a disappointment. They'd all rather have had him than me.

The train was slowing, the brakes dragging harder, the blur outside gradually re-forming into the blackened backs of terraced houses, splicing into warehouses, office towers, and finally the iron of bridges and railway station. We had reached London.

I began to stuff my things back into my rucksack. I would run away for good and solve everyone's problems. Try and get by in London. I could get a job. Doors were hissing again. The old lady got off, other people were getting on.

I didn't move. I just couldn't make the final decision. Who was I kidding? I couldn't make it alone in London. I didn't want to. All I wanted was a happy family. Peace and space to get on with being me.

A group of three guys and a girl surged towards me, laughing, shoving at each other, chucking bags into the luggage holds and flopping one by one into the bay across the aisle.

'Aaaaaaarg!' groaned the guy with the shaved head. 'Can I get rid of this hangover in time for the Nuclear Fission lecture?'

'Think your atoms have already split, mate!' said the girl. Everyone howled laughing.

As the laughter built, something made me turn to look at the girl. Her black hair was braided tight against her head in an incredible geometric pattern, like a maze. She caught me staring. And then she stared back and I realized, with a sinking feeling, that we knew each other. The last thing I needed! The very worst thing that could happen now!

I quickly looked away. How did we know each other? Where from? My brain was still scrabbling frantically when she said, 'It's Dominic, isn't it? Carla Gordon's son?'

She swung across to the seat opposite mine.

'Wooooo!' yelled one of the guys with her. 'Zita's found a toy-boy!'

My face burned as they laughed. Zita. Yes, that was her name. Zita.

'Ignore them,' she smiled. 'Don't you remember me? Zita Robinson? Your mum used to give me singing lessons. Couple of years ago now.'

And now I remembered that wide, warm smile and the outrageous laugh that often used to follow it. She'd been a really good singer too, I remembered Mum saying so.

'Yes, I do remember. Hello,' I said. Perhaps this wouldn't be too bad. I needn't say I was going to Cambridge.

'Where are you heading?' she asked.

'Ummm . . . just on a sort of a project.' I looked out of the window.

'You know, it's great that I've met you on a train to Cambridge,' she said.

'Is it?' I said. I turned back to see her beaming at me.

'Yes, because it's all down to your wonderful, beautiful mother that I'm here. It's thanks to her that I got my music scholarship. I'm studying at Cambridge now. She was a really good teacher. It's a shame she gave it up. How is she nowadays?'

'She's fine,' I said.

'Good. So . . . you didn't say where you were heading.'

'Um, well, actually I'm going to Cambridge too. For this project,' I said.

'Great place, you'll love it,' she said. 'What's the project?'

'Well, I'm trying to find out about . . . about a relative who once studied there. But it's a secret project. I don't want to tell my mum and dad about it yet.' This was no lie, after all.

'Ooooh,' she said. 'Your secret's safe with me! Hey, you want anything?'

I tore my eyes away from her face and saw the refreshment trolley heading towards us.

'Let me. I've got sundry beverages on my ticket.' I grinned.

'Have you, now?' She laughed. 'Student tickets don't cover such luxuries.'

I flashed the ticket and got us both Cokes. It was getting hotter. Outside, a rippling blanket of bright corn was flying by, dry and dusty. It looked as if it would burst into flames at any moment.

'Too hot to go back to work,' said Zita.

'Why do you have to?' I asked. 'I thought students got really long summer holidays.'

'It depends,' she said. 'You can choose to work right through the holiday if the course you want is available. Mine is, and if I can pass this one nightmare of an exam over the summer there'll be less pressure next year. I'm trying to get ahead of the game.'

'Oh,' I said. 'That would explain why my father wants me to go to Cambridge. A place where I'd have to spend every waking hour slaving over exams—nothing would please him more!'

Zita threw back her head and laughed the ringing, chuckling laugh that I remembered coming from Mum's music room in the days when she still had a music room. It was the sort of laugh that made you laugh with her, and I did.

'So. Which college did this relative go to?' she asked.

'He went to the university,' I said. 'The university of Cambridge. That's all I know.'

'That's *all* you know?'

I nodded.

She shook her head. 'Then you've got your work cut out. The university is made up of lots of different colleges. You need to find out which college, and ask there.'

I stared at her in panic. 'But I don't know!'

'How long ago was he there?'

'Umm . . . quite some time ago.'

'OK,' she said, studying me with her almost-black eyes. 'Which subject did he study?'

'Something to do with sciences. But . . . ' I tried to remember if there'd been any mention of which college he'd been at, but I just didn't know. I hadn't been looking out for that sort of thing. 'I've seen a photo that I think must have been taken in Cambridge—well, he would have been the right age for university, I think, when it was taken. He was leaning against an old wall near a river. There were some bicycles . . . '

Zita leaned forward. 'Do you have the photo with you?'

'No.'

'Your only clue and you left it behind?'

I glared out of the window. She was right. It was stupid. The whole idea was just stupid. I was chasing after something that couldn't be found.

'Hey.' She patted my hand. 'I'm sorry. Don't give up on it. This photo—what was he wearing?'

'Um . . . it was winter. Jeans. A long coat . . . a scarf.'

'What colours were on the scarf?'

'Blue, I think, and . . . I can't remember. Why?'

She smiled. 'Cambridge is full of old walls and bicycles, as you'll see when you get there. What you gotta home in on is that scarf. Each college has its own colours. The colours of the scarf will tell you his college.'

'But I can't remember the colours!'

I felt the drag of the train's brakes.

'Nearly there,' said Zita.

'No! I've got to remember!'

She got up and pulled a bag from the luggage hold. She rummaged and found a notebook and pen.

'Everything that goes into your brain stays there. You've just got to find a way of unlocking it,' she said.

'What d'you mean?'

'I mean, there's this theory that you *can* remember if you get the right stimulus. Go to the university outfitters, look at the scarves. It might just jog the memory cells. Let me know how you get on—it'd be a really interesting experiment.'

She scribbled down an address. 'It's easy to find. I don't have a town map, I'm afraid, but you can buy one at the kiosk in the ticket hall. Hey, look, why don't we meet up for lunch after my tutorial? There's a place two doors up from the outfitters.'

She grabbed at the seat back as the train slid to a stop.

'So you can see if the experiment works?' I said.

'Exactly.' She grinned. 'Look, we gotta run, or we'll be late for the tutorial. You'll find your way around OK?'

'Yeah, I'll be fine. And, Zita—it *is* a secret project.'

'My lips are sealed!' She laughed. 'See you one o'clock-ish. Good luck!'

8

I headed for the rack of cards and maps at the kiosk in the booking hall. The crowd of students from the station was thinning and by the time I'd chosen a map there was hardly anyone around. Just a woman with some kids and a blonde lady in a lilac suit. I noticed her because of the lilac. It was a beautiful colour.

The next time I looked up I noticed her again, nearer. She was standing at a communications booth, but she wasn't using it and didn't look as if she was going to. What she was doing was staring at me.

Perhaps she thought I was nicking stuff. With a flourish, I took my wallet from my back pocket and handed over the money for a map. She was still staring. Nosy cow. I got my change and headed out of the station.

There was the usual bike park and a bike and electrocar hire place, just like any other station. A few taxis and one private car with tinted glass. People were streaming away on bikes—some pedal bikes, some electric, with their motors whining on the hot air. I glanced at my map. The town centre didn't look far, and in any case I couldn't read a map and ride a bike at the same time. So I set off walking.

Straight away you could see this was an old, old city. The roofs had chimneys instead of solar tiles. The shapes and colours of the buildings were all so different from the drab sameness of the New Towns in the south. They were all so different from each other too. There were black bricks and red bricks and honey-coloured stone, weird little turrets and diamond-paned windows. It was like being in a fairy tale.

I strolled along, drinking it all in, enjoying the sunshine and the feeling of being free. It was strange how good I felt here. At home. It was as if this place had been waiting for me to find it. The churning, jealous feelings about my brother all slipped away and I could almost feel him leading me, showing me his city. I didn't bother with the map. I just walked.

I came to the end of a narrow lane and suddenly saw, dead ahead, a building that stopped me, made me gasp out loud. It was like a carved mountain, with sheer walls rearing up into little pinnacles and a massive stained-glass window in the end facing me. There was a sound rumbling deep inside the building. Dodging the bikes, I ran across the road and stood listening.

It was organ music, so deep and powerful that it seemed the building itself was singing. And then a choir came in, softly at first—a male voice choir singing something that seemed vaguely familiar.

I listened until the music stopped and the noise of the real world rushed back in. Chattering tourists, students, and grizzling kids swept past me. My hands felt numb, and I realized that I had been gripping too hard on to the iron rail in front of me. Suddenly, I remembered what I was supposed to be doing and looked around to see which street I was on.

By chance, I had come to exactly where I was supposed to be. Across the street was an ancient-looking shop called Arnold Cricket, University Outfitters. I dodged the bikes again and went in.

The shop was full of the smell of polished wood and new clothes. On one wall there was a huge wooden cabinet that went from floor to ceiling. It was stuffed with brightly-coloured scarves, neatly rolled.

'May we help you, sir?' A thin man bounded up to me. He had a startled sort of face, glasses, and a tuft of hair sticking up on his head. He smiled the sort of smile you had to smile back at. I decided to come clean.

'I'm on a mission,' I said.

'Ooooooh!' His eyebrows shot up above his glasses.

I explained. He listened carefully and when I'd finished he said, 'I think your friend's right. You have a good look round and maybe you'll remember. Take them out and drape them about if you want to. Festoon the place. Don't mind me!'

He smiled, bounded back to the counter, and left me to it.

I studied the wall of scarves, picking out the ones that had blue in them. There was a blue and purple combination that seemed familiar. But I knew that my brother's scarf had had three colours. Blue, purple, and . . . I closed my eyes and concentrated hard on my memory of the photo. Yes, purple felt right. And the third colour was a pale colour. Suddenly I knew. I opened my eyes and searched the wall of scarves again. The amazing thing was, I'd seen the colour very recently. It was lilac. That wonderful colour that the nosy lady in the station had been wearing.

And there it was, a blue, purple, and lilac scarf, near the top of the wall! I called the man and told him. He seemed almost as excited as I was.

'Ooooh, that's Grenville Hall!' he cried. 'Well done! Are you sure, now?'

'I'm certain,' I said. 'Zita was right!'

'The mysteries of the human brain!' said the man.

Grenville Hall, I said over and over in my head. I'd found his college. I was getting nearer.

After all that, I felt I should buy something. I wanted to, anyway. A souvenir. No, more than that—something

41

real to connect me with my brother. I wanted to wear something that he might have worn.

'Do you do T-shirts?' I asked.

'You mean, do we stock a sports shirt,' said the man.

'Do I?'

'Yes, sir, you most definitely mean the sports shirt.' He smiled. 'With the Grenville Hall badge, I take it?'

He showed me the shirt in several different colours and I chose a red and a white one and handed over my Jiddy card. I spread my map on the counter and looked for Grenville Hall.

'It's not far,' said the man. The map had little pictures of various buildings, and he pointed to one of them. 'There.'

'Wow! It's one of the really old-fashioned ones!' I cried.

'Draughty in the winter,' said the man. 'Loads of ghosts.'

'Yeah, right!' I laughed.

At that moment I happened to glance through the window behind the counter and there was the lilac lady again, only feet away outside, looking at the window display. She was quite pretty for a Mum's-age woman, her bright blonde hair glinting in the sun. I smiled at her even though she wasn't looking at me. She deserved a smile because she had, in a way, been my lucky talisman.

9

I had half an hour before I was due to meet up with Zita so I decided to begin the next step of the mission by finding Grenville Hall.

I looked at the map and found a route that took me through narrow side-streets where cyclists weaved around pedestrians and the thick stone walls of the buildings echoed with the sound of bicycle bells. I glanced up as yet another bell sounded, a clock bell this time, striking quarter to one. The clock was set in a huge brick archway with two towers, like the entrance to a castle. It looked familiar and I suddenly realized that I had arrived. This was Grenville Hall.

The archway was filled by massive wooden doors, weather-beaten and studded with iron, but there was a smaller door cut into one side of the big doors. I shivered in the shade under the archway. And then I saw the notice:

NOT OPEN TO THE PUBLIC

But that didn't include me. I had a right to be here. I strode towards the little arched door and almost had my hand on the iron ring when someone said, 'Oi there! Sonny Jim!'

I swung round to see an old bloke at a sort of serving hatch in the stone wall next to the archway. He had a face like a bulldog. I just knew he was going to say 'Where d'you think you're going?'

He cleared his throat.

'Where d'you think you're going?' he said.

'Umm . . . I've come to look round. My brother was here and . . .'

'Not today, sonny. Prize-giving day. Students and guests only today.'

'But my brother . . .'

'Has he won a prize?'

'Yes, loads,' I said.

He looked at me. I was pretty sure he knew I was trying to spin him a line.

'Can I have your name then, sonny, and the name of your brother?'

'Dominic Gordon . . .'

'And your brother's name?' He was looking at a list. I knew I'd blown it now.

'Er . . . no, that *is* my brother's name. I'm Michael,' I mumbled.

'So we're looking for a Dominic Gordon?'

'Yes, but . . . he might not be on the list.'

He puffed out his saggy cheeks and snapped shut the book with the list. 'You're quite right, he's not. No Gordons at all.'

'But I've *got* to get in!' I cried.

'This place was built in 'Enery the Eighth's time, sonny. It'll still be here if you come back tomorrow.' He wobbled his chins at me. 'Run along now.'

I turned away, feeling stupid, and strode to the other side of the street. When I glanced back he was still watching me, like a dog guarding its home.

I stared at the great gateway. I imagined my brother going through that little oak door and then, suddenly, I imagined Mum and Dad coming here to collect the body of their brilliant son, their only child.

A bell jangled close behind me.

'Get outa the road, mate!' A cyclist swerved round me.

'Sorry!'

I stepped onto the pavement and made my way back towards the outfitters. A couple of doors along I found the café Zita had told me about. The door jangled as I opened it to see a long, low room packed with chattering students. The rich cooking smells hit me and my mouth instantly watered. I realized that I'd missed supper last night and the executive breakfast hadn't done much to fill the hole. Down at the far end of the café someone was waving and I saw Zita's braided head.

'Well?' she asked as I flopped into the chair opposite her.

'You were right,' I said. 'I found it. Grenville Hall.'

I told her how I'd remembered two of the scarf's colours for myself and had then had a bit of help from the lilac lady.

'That's fascinating,' said Zita. 'As a result of the right stimulus, you've recalled a subliminal image.'

'Yes, but I wouldn't have known how to do it—where to go, I mean, unless you'd told me,' I said.

'True,' she grinned. 'Nevertheless it was a worthwhile experiment. You hungry?'

'Ravenous.'

I saw a guy on the next table tucking into a huge pie with mash and peas and I ordered the same.

'I can't get into Grenville Hall today, though,' I explained.

'Of course! Prize-giving,' said Zita. 'I can't help, I'm afraid, I don't know anyone who lives there.'

'Is there any other way in?' I asked. 'Could I climb over a wall or something?'

'Only if you want to break your neck or get into trouble with the bursar—or both. It should be open again tomorrow. If you need to stay over you can crash at our place—there's loads of space because some people have gone off for the summer already.'

45

'Really? Thanks.' It felt odd, having someone treat me as a responsible, grown-up person for a change.

'No problem. Like I said, I respected Carla and she did me proud,' she said. 'Consider it a small token of my appreciation if I can help you at all. So are you going to tell me about this mystery relative? What's so special about him?'

'Well, like I said, it's . . . .' I looked up at her, saw her eyes wide and thoughtful. It wasn't that she was being nosy. She sensed something was wrong. And she might help me if I was brave enough to open up. Anyway, I wanted to. I wanted to share this, to talk to someone. 'It's my brother. He died before I was born,' I said.

It felt so weird, to have someone I could call 'my' and yet I knew nothing about him.

'Oh, Dominic!' She stretched out a hand to mine. 'That's really sad! Your poor parents!'

'Yes. They don't know I'm here, though. It's just something . . . something I had to do.'

'So—have you always known you had this brother?' she asked.

'No. Found out yesterday,' I said.

'And you don't have any other brothers and sisters, do you, if I remember right?'

I shook my head. I found myself playing with the salt and pepper pots, twiddling them round and round. It wasn't easy to explain to myself, let alone anyone else. And it felt so strange to be doing all this, trying to track down a piece of the past.

'I want to find out how he died,' I said. 'And . . . and what he was like.'

Zita smiled. 'Well, I think that's great. And I'll help you all I can.'

Our food came. We both started eating.

46

'I suppose I need to find someone who remembers him,' I said. 'If anyone does.'

'That may not be too difficult,' said Zita. 'It's quite possible that you'll find a tutor who remembers him or, if you're lucky, a friend who's stayed on as part of the academic staff—quite a few do, and it can't be that long ago, can it? Do you know when he was here?'

'Between 1999 and 2001. I suppose that means he died sometime in 2001.'

Saying the dates aloud made me realize something.

'We only just missed each other,' I said. 'I was born on New Year's Day 2002.'

My throat had tightened. I couldn't swallow my mouthful of pie. I chewed hard and blinked the dampness out of my eyes, hoping she wouldn't notice.

We finished eating in silence. At last, Zita said quietly, 'I'm an only child too. It must be a lot for you to come to terms with, when you've been an only child all your life. I'm so used to it being just me, my mom and dad—no one else who comes from them like I do. I think I'd find it tough to know that my parents had another child—even tougher if I could never know him.'

I nodded at my plate.

'Look,' she said, delving into her bag. 'Here's my address and phone number. If you want to give me a call, you can work on the computer at our place if you need to. I'll be back there later this afternoon. Did you get a map?'

'Yes.'

'Right then, you might find something at the library, but I'm not sure how much access you can get without a student card. I've got to go—I'm meeting up with my summer tutor. You take it easy, now. Ring me either way. Let me know how you get on.'

'Thanks, Zita.'

She shoved the address card into my hand and patted

47

my shoulder as she brushed past. I stared after her as she paid the bill and left the café, stepping out onto the crowded street, the great cathedral-like building dominating the skyline behind her.

My brother had been a student like her, like all these students around me. Perhaps he had even eaten in this café. I pushed my plate away.

I'm going to find you, I told him in my head. I'm going to find you.

10

The university library was easy to find from its drawing on the map. It looked a bit like the old power station in London that had been turned into the Tate Modern and I remembered with a pang that Mum had taken me there last Easter when Dad was away on a business trip.

I pushed through the heavy revolving door. Behind the reception desk was a young woman with spiky green hair and to her left was a row of barriers like the ones you go through at a railway station. I waited at the desk while the receptionist finished writing something. She looked up and smiled.

'Can I help you?'

'I wanted to look something up. In the library,' I said.

'Are you a student?' she asked.

'No.'

'I'm sorry, I'm afraid the only parts of the library open to the public are the coffee bars and the exhibition halls. "Three Centuries of Doll-making" or "East Anglian Thatching".'

'Sorry?'

'Those are the exhibitions currently running.'

'Oh,' I said.

'What was it you were after?'

I explained what I needed.

'Easy,' she said. 'Go on to the university website. Find College Pages and then Yearbooks. The Grenville Hall Yearbook for that year will give you a list of the people at

49

Grenville Hall at the right time. But you'll need more than that, because people in each college study all sorts of different subjects in different faculties. The college is only where they live . . . '

'And they sort of . . . go to school at these different faculties?' I said.

'You got it—so he'd probably have had friends in both Grenville and his faculty. So to find the list for the faculty you go to the Faculty Yearbook. Once you've got all the names you could do a search to see if any of your brother's contemporaries are still here on the university teaching staff. That could take some time, though.'

'OK—that's a real help, thanks!'

'That's what library staff are for.' She smiled and handed me a card. 'Here's the university website address.'

I was on my way back to the revolving door when she called out to me.

'Hey, hang on! If you want to wait five minutes, there may be a computer booth available in there.' She nodded towards a room just off the foyer. 'That way you can go straight through to the university database. You might as well give it five, if you're not in a hurry.'

'OK, thanks.'

I wandered over to a window seat and spread out my map. Once I'd got the information I needed, I might do some exploring and then go and call in on Zita. I studied the index to see if there was an Art faculty.

A sudden banging and rattling at one of the barriers made me look up. There was a blonde woman, smartly dressed in a grey suit, trying to get through.

'Stupid thing!' she cried.

She marched over to the receptionist, her high heels spiking the stone floor.

'My card won't go through! You'll have to open the barrier for me!'

'I'm afraid it's expired,' said the receptionist, looking at the card. 'Graduate cards need to be renewed every five years.'

'Well then, just look up my name and renew it,' snapped the blonde woman. 'My name's Leanne Kelsey. And I haven't got all day!'

'Do you have identification?'

'Oh, for God's sake! Just look up my name! I'm a well-known graduate of this university. It's not as if nobody knows who I am around here!'

A porter stepped forward. 'I'll let Miss Kelsey through,' he said. 'I know who she is.'

'Thank YOU!' said the woman, pushing through the barrier as the porter unlocked it. She nearly had his arm off.

The porter shook his head as she stomped away. 'We know *her* all right!' he said to the girl at the desk.

'There shouldn't be one rule for her and another for everyone else!' said the receptionist, swiping a hand angrily through her spikes of green hair.

A buzzer sounded and a red light flashed on a board behind her. She glanced across at me. 'There's a computer free now—through you go. I'll have to ask you to move if a student needs it but you should have enough time to get those lists.'

'Thanks!' I went into the room at the side of the foyer and found the desk that had just been vacated. I got into the university database and followed the instructions the receptionist had given me. I found the Grenville Hall lists for 1999, 2000, and 2001. Some of the names changed, and I supposed that was because people were in different years, but my brother's name was there for all three years. It also said he was in the Life Sciences Faculty, as I'd found from my first search at home. I printed up the lists and then went to the Life Sciences Faculty pages. The list of students studying at the same time as my brother was pages long. I decided to print it up first, just in case I was turfed out of here, and while it was printing I found my brother's name. Beneath it was the list of prizes again, ending with the Professor Holt Prize for most Outstanding Undergraduate Work in Life Sciences. I flumped back crossly in the chair. Of all my failures in my father's eyes, my failures in the sciences were the worst. But as well as resenting my brother, I felt proud of him. It was a strange, uncomfortable mixture of feeling and I didn't want it. I wriggled on the chair and kicked at the desk.

'Hey,' said a voice behind me, 'if you've finished demolishing the place, I'll have that computer. When you're ready.'

There was a huge bloke standing over me, clutching a bundle of files. Chest like a rugby player. And a crooked nose, so he probably was a rugby player.

'Time waits for no man,' he said. 'What are you printing there, the London phone directory?'

'Sorry,' I said. 'It won't take long.'

'You're right there,' he said. And he leant over, clicked cancel on the print operation and pulled back the chair, with me still on it.

'There we go.' He handed me my papers as I stood up.

'Thanks,' I said lamely. 'Sorry.'

I scuttled back to my window seat in the foyer and looked through the print-ups. I'd got all the Grenville Hall stuff and six pages of the Life Science Faculty. The other stuff I'd have to get at Zita's. I packed the print-ups away in my rucksack and got out my map to look up her address. It wasn't far and I could walk along the river bank for part of the way. The map crackled noisily as I struggled to fold it the way I needed it, and when I eventually got it right I caught an icy stare from a woman behind the reception desk. My green-haired friend was gone and this new woman obviously didn't like people crackling in her foyer. I reckoned it was time to go.

It turned out that there were only three more pages of names in the Life Sciences Faculty. Zita and I spent most of the rest of the day back at her place getting a list of the teaching staff and cross-referencing names with the lists we already had to find out if there was anyone from my brother's time still here in Cambridge.

There were three names to go on. Two people from my brother's time were now researchers at the Life Sciences Faculty under the leadership of Professor Holt. Another, Dr Giles Nickalls, was a tutor in the Ecology Faculty.

'It's a shame, but I don't think you'll get near anyone from Professor Holt's team,' said Zita. 'I'm afraid your timing's not great—there's a huge medical conference beginning the day after tomorrow and I reckon they'll all be tied up with that. But Dr Nickalls—you could try him. It looks as though he's your best bet anyway—he hasn't moved far in sixteen years, he's still in the same study. Look!'

She pointed to some letters and numbers on the Grenville Hall list that I hadn't taken much notice of.

'D3—that means he's in room 3 on D staircase, same as he was in 2000. Your brother was in room 4!'

'So they could have been mates?'

'Well, let's just say they might have known each other.'

'Great! That's where I'll go tomorrow!'

While Zita made us some food, I chilled out in the cluttered front room. There were five students in this house and the room looked as if it had bits from all their lives— a cricket bat, a music stand, a collection of really awful turn-of-the-century CDs and a life-size model of a human brain. There was also a cheese sandwich, now wearing a blue fur coat, that had been there for seven weeks, Zita said.

One of the students was making notes about the stages of its decomposition.

I could imagine myself living like this. In a house with friends, doing interesting things, having the space and time to work and study.

'I'd like to go to university,' I told Zita, as she handed me a plate of beans on toast and settled herself on the sofa beside me. 'I want to study Art.'

'Great idea,' she said. 'There are university courses or Art Colleges. Whatever suits you best.'

Whatever suits me best, I thought to myself as I went to sleep that night in a complete stranger's room. I'd never looked at it that way before.

11

In the morning I dashed out early to a little shop I'd noticed on the corner of Zita's street. I wanted to get us something for breakfast, and something for her. In the end I settled on eggs, muffins, and a box of chocolates.

'That's sweet of you!' she cried when I gave her the things.

'No, it's nothing. You've been a good friend,' I said.

'You're off home today then, once you've tried to find this Dr Nickalls?'

'Maybe. It depends what I find.'

'Well, you know you can always stay here again if you need to—you've got my number, right?'

'Right,' I smiled.

We sat in her sunny back garden to have a breakfast of scrambled eggs and muffins, then I packed up my stuff and said goodbye. As I stood on the pavement, swinging my rucksack onto my back, with Zita leaning in the doorway of the old terraced house, she suddenly said, 'Whatever you're looking for, I hope you find it.'

'So do I.' I grinned up at her. 'And thanks—you've been almost like a sister!'

She burst out laughing. 'Sister? Yeah, right! Off you go!'

And I set off down the street, turning at the corner to wave at her.

When I reached the gateway in the Grenville Hall towers, old bulldog-face was nowhere to be seen. The notice was gone and so I assumed I could just walk in. I was a few paces away from the little door when the hatch in the wall opened and there he was. He looked quite pleased to see me.

'It's you again,' he said helpfully.

'I've come to see Dr Giles Nickalls. Staircase D, room 3,' I said.

'Mmmmm.' He pursed his lips and scrunched his forehead into deep furrows. 'Not sure about that, sonny.'

'Fine,' I said. 'If you won't let me in, I'll find another way!'

I stomped off into the bright, hot street.

'Oi!' he called after me. 'Don't go flouncing off! I thought it was your brother you wanted to see.'

'No, I want to see Dr Nickalls.'

'Don't think he's here. Think he left yesterday,' he said, disappearing through his hatch into a tiny office set in the thick wall of the archway.

'What?'

He came back with a big red ledger.

'No,' he said, 'Dr Nickalls has gone. Signed out yesterday afternoon for the summer break.'

'Damn!'

'Language!' he said.

I drew breath to tell him to shut up, but thought better of it. As the disappointment and frustration swilled around inside me, I tried to think if there was anything else I could do.

'Is there anybody else here who was here sixteen years ago?' I asked.

'Wouldn't know. I've only been here ten,' he said.

I sighed. 'OK. Can I go in anyway?'

'Be my guest,' he said. 'It's a free country.'

And so, at last, I was allowed to step through the little wooden door into the dazzling sunlight. In front of me was a brick pathway leading across a grassy square. On all four sides, old buildings leaned and sagged. One side was timbered—from the time of Elizabeth I, or perhaps just made to look as if it was. Ahead there was crumbling red brick and to the right you could hardly make out what the building was made of—just the odd bit of pale stone and some diamond-paned windows showing amongst the ivy. The whole place seemed to be ticking at a slower speed, taking no notice of the outside world at all, sure of its history, sure that it would always be here. Even if I couldn't find anything here to help me, at least I'd seen it and felt it, I thought. I stepped out to walk down the path he must have walked down.

A sudden whirring sound behind me cut into the silence and set my heart racing. Before I could turn, a girl on a bike sped past me and disappeared through the red-brick archway ahead. You could see green meadows through the arch, and willows. The river! I'd go and look later, see if I could find the bridge where the photo of my brother was taken. Perhaps I could even find a tutor—somebody, anybody, to ask if they'd known him.

But for now I wanted to find D staircase and the room where my brother had lived. I could see that there were archways leading to staircases at various points around the square. I followed the path around and found D staircase, a spiral of worn stone steps twisting up into musty half-light. I could see dark, heavy wooden doors leading off the staircase. I climbed up to room 3 and found Dr Nickalls's name. I paused, then knocked anyway, just in case.

I fidgeted around, waiting in the deep silence and the chill that seeped from the thick stone walls. I didn't really expect anything to happen. I looked above me and could just make out what must be the bottom of the fourth door. The room where my brother had lived.

I turned back to Dr Nickalls's door. He wasn't there, of course he wasn't. Probably on his way to some exotic holiday. I went on, a few steps further up the staircase, just to see my brother's door.

I stood in front of it and took hold of the pitted iron ring. So many hands must have used it over the centuries. I just wanted to feel one hand. I wanted to open the door and find him there. But the iron was cold and I shivered so violently that my hand snatched from the ring and it fell back against the wood with a dead thud.

And then I heard the shuffle of footsteps below. I moved away from the door and glanced down the stairwell. There was a man, youngish, with thick gingery hair, jingling keys at Dr Nickalls's door.

12

'Excuse me,' I called down the staircase, 'are you Dr Nickalls?'

I went down the steps towards him.

'My name's Dominic Gordon.'

The man glanced up and his gasp echoed down the stairwell. A word slipped from him in a whisper but I couldn't make out what it was. He was staring, white-faced. And then I realized what the problem might be.

'I've come about my brother,' I said. 'I know I look like him. And we've got the same name. I was just having a look at his door. Did you know him?'

'Dominic's brother?' gasped the man.

'Yes,' I said, flooding with relief. 'Are you Dr Nickalls?'

'Yes, I'm Dr Nickalls.' He took a step towards me and then hesitated. 'Good God!' he breathed.

He swung back to the door and began fiddling with the keys.

'You'd better come in, come in,' he mumbled. 'Place is a bit of a mess, but um . . .'

I followed him through the arched doorway.

The room was dark, with small, diamond-paned windows at either end. There was a whole wall of books, as well as books piled on tables, on the windowsills, on the floor, even on the chairs.

'Ha . . . thing is,' said Dr Nickalls, 'the cleaners have rather given up on me. I make too much dust. Just can't seem to keep things . . .' He flipped back his heavy, gingery fringe and stared at me again.

'Cup of tea?' he said at last, lurching towards a little sink at the back of the room.

'Yeah, thanks,' I said. 'Did you know my brother well?'

He dropped the lid of the kettle. We waited while it rang circles on the hard floor. He bent to pick it up.

'He was my best friend,' he said.

He sniffed and shot a hand up to his face.

'Are your parents with you?' he asked, his voice bright and wobbly.

'No, and they don't know I'm here,' I said.

'Oh.' He looked surprised. 'So . . . what have they told you about him?'

'Just that he died here in Cambridge. I'd never have known about him at all if I hadn't accidentally found a photo album the day before yesterday. They never told me I had a brother.'

'The day before yesterday? So you've seen a photo?'

'Yes, we look quite a lot like each other, don't we?'

'And have you met anyone else in Cambridge?'

'No.' I shrugged. 'You're the first person I've tried.'

He spun round with a smile.

'Call me Giles,' he said. 'I think I've got some biscuits somewhere.'

He faffed around, hair flopping over his face as he cleared somewhere to sit, found biscuits, and made the tea. I sank into a dusty armchair. I wondered if, all those years ago, my brother's room above us had been like this. You never saw a room full of books now. It suddenly seemed so exciting, to live in a room full of books. Perhaps I could make a room like this if I went to university.

'Go on, help yourself,' said Giles.

'Thanks.' I took a mug of tea.

'Hope you don't mind my asking,' he said, 'but . . . how old are you?'

'Fifteen,' I said.

He nodded.

I needed to fill the silence, so I said, 'We'd have met if I'd been born a year earlier.'

A stupid thing to say. Giles looked puzzled.

The question burst out before I meant it to: 'What happened to him?'

'He was knocked off his bike,' said Giles. 'Taken to the hospital unconscious. And then he came round and he was fine. Sitting up in bed demanding to be taken home because he had an essay to finish. And then, that night, he just died.'

'How? If he was all right?'

'A blood clot. He'd hit his head quite hard, you see.'

Another silence. I started to prattle on.

'He was doing science, wasn't he? Now I know why my father's always been so heavy with me about my science grades. I'm no good at it and he's disappointed because my brother was a genius. Well, my father's a genius too, so I suppose they were just disappointed all round, really . . .'

Giles leaned forward in his chair and frowned at the floor. At last he looked up. 'What makes you think your father is disappointed with you?' he asked.

'He's always going on about it. How much they pay for my school and how slow I am at understanding things. I thought he just hated the fact that I wasn't like him, but now it looks like it wasn't only that. Maybe he hates the fact that I'm not like my brother.'

Giles sighed. 'You shouldn't compare yourself with him,' he said. 'You know, your father's very wrong if he puts that sort of pressure on you.'

As soon as he said that, something awful happened. My eyes went hot and wet and a great gulp snatched at my throat. Just to hear someone say it. After all the times I'd

61

been made to feel that who I was and what I was good at counted for nothing. Just to hear someone say it wasn't me, it was my father who was wrong.

Giles came to sit on the arm of my chair and patted me gently on the back. I felt stupid. But I couldn't help it.

'I'm sorry,' I sniffed.

'Don't be sorry,' said Giles. 'You've had a bad shock, suddenly finding out like that. Only the day before yesterday, you said?'

I nodded.

I saw him look at his watch. I ought to go! He was probably busy and I was taking up his time.

'Look,' he said, 'I have to pop out for half an hour or so, but when I come back we can get out of here, have a proper chat.'

'Thanks,' I snivelled.

'Meanwhile,' he said, 'have a look through this.' He rooted about in one of the bookshelves and came back with a photo album. 'It'll give you some idea of Nick's life here.' He flicked through the pages and smiled sadly. 'He was a great friend, great fun to be with. And if it's any consolation, I think he'd be bowled over by the idea of having a brother, if he could know.'

He smiled and then swung round and out of the door.

I held the album in shaking hands. And then I opened it.

They were all there, my family, living in their secret history. Mum and my brother leaning against that same stone bridge, squinting into the sun. He had an arm draped around her shoulder and, with that churning feeling again, I saw that she looked so happy, full of an energy that I'd never seen in her before. And my father, smiling again, just as he had in the pictures I'd seen in Pops's attic.

I stared at my brother, at this face that was so like me, and yet not me. 'Nick', as Giles had called him, and I was glad that, although we'd been given the same name, we weren't both called the same. Had he had problems with my father—our father—too? Didn't look like it. They all looked like the happiest people in the world.

There were notes in neat handwriting: 'Easter 1999', and 'Nick shows us how to punt', below a picture of my brother stretched between a punt and its pole, which was stuck upright in the river.

It looked like a great life. Parties, girls, beer, picnics. A younger version of Giles with a pair of knickers on his head, and three bare bums sticking out of a window—no caption for those. There was a blonde girl who seemed to be Nick's girlfriend. In most of the photos she was giggling. Then there was Nick with a different girl, this time much prettier and dark-haired. Another neat caption told me her name was Becky.

The photos stopped suddenly before the end of the album. The last one was of my brother standing alone by a river. He was staring out of the photo straight at me, looking thoughtful. I imagined myself stepping into the photo, the two of us strolling down the path by the river and talking. I caught his eye again. I shivered. A photo is a moment in time that you can never have back. And you can't ask questions of dead people, you can only guess what's locked inside the picture.

I closed the album, lay back, and shut my eyes. Why hadn't they told me? Why hide twenty-one years—a whole life?

There was a sudden rap on the door. I jumped and the album fell off my lap with a thud, shooting a couple more photos across the floor. The person rapped again. Perhaps I should take a message. But then I might have to explain who I was and what I was doing here, and I didn't fancy that.

And then the iron door-latch twitched upwards. But

there was an old Yale too, so whoever it was couldn't get in. I waited for them to go away, then went to the window, thinking I'd better see who it was so that I could tell Giles.

I knelt on the window seat and waited for the person to come down the staircase. A few seconds later, someone stepped from the building and walked briskly across the courtyard. Her hair shone in the midday sun. It was the lilac lady again.

13

As I watched her walk away I had a really strange feeling. I suddenly felt I knew her. Everything about her seemed familiar—her quick, decisive way of walking, her slim shape, the neat sweep of hair. And then, like a lost memory, the feeling was gone. I looked at her again and saw an unknown woman in a lilac suit walking through the archway that led to the river.

I slumped on the window seat and closed my eyes again. Giles was right, I was in shock. I tried to let my mind go blank but things kept swirling into it. Parties and picnics and mucking about on the river. I could hear laughter, the splashing of oars. I could smell mown grass and beer. I could see the laughing face of the dark-haired girl, Becky.

I opened my eyes and tried to concentrate on everyday things in the room. I wasn't going mad, was I? Chairs, kettle, books, chairs, kettle, books . . . I tried to shake the visions of my brother's life, but I couldn't shake the feelings. They hung just out of reach in my mind, like feelings you try to remember from a dream.

I glanced at the album on the floor. Some photos had fallen out of it. I picked up the album and the stray photos and found that the ones that had fallen out when she had knocked on the door weren't photos after all. They were a couple of postcards that must have been tucked into the back of the album. I looked at the cosy country scene on the first postcard. Then I turned it over, immediately looking for the writer's name. It was signed Nick. He had awful handwriting.

'Giles, you old gibbon, hurry up and pass those re-sits and get yourself down here. Pops has been taking us flying and it's FANTASTIC! It turns out that Becky has a talent for it (flying, I mean!!) and Pops has let her take the controls already. Mum and Dad and Pops and Gran think Becky's wonderful, of course. Please don't think you'll be a gooseberry, because you won't be—we all want you here, so GET ON WITH IT! Nick.'

I gripped the card with trembling hands. This was better than photos. I could hear his voice in my head. I wanted more. I flipped over the second postcard. But this one wasn't from him. It was Mum's writing.

Dearest Giles,

I have never written to thank you for your kindness when Nick died. Please forgive me, but things have been terrible these last few weeks. As you can see, we are now in the Cayman Islands at the generous invitation of Professor Holt, who is here doing some research and kindly felt that the break might do us good. In a way it is of some comfort to be close to someone who knew Nick so well—but in other ways, as you can imagine, it is painful.

My husband is talking of selling up and starting a new life in the States. I don't want to go, but then, I don't really want to be anywhere.

Thank you for being such a good friend to my son. I know he thought the world of you. I wish you happiness always, dear Giles.

All my love, Carla.

I wanted to hug Mum. I wanted to wrap her up and stop her from ever hurting again. And I wanted her to wrap me up and stop me from hurting. Why couldn't we do that? Why hadn't we ever been able to do that? And why the hell had my father made her go to the States when she would have needed Pops and Gran? Why had he spent his whole damned life only thinking of what *he* wanted?

And who exactly was Professor Holt? The same Professor Holt that had given my brother a prize? It must be.

Something was scrabbling and clicking at the door and I slapped the album shut as Giles bounded in.

He paused for a moment, looking at me in that half-nervous way.

'Right you are, then,' he smiled. 'Enough of being cooped up here. Picnic lunch, how's that?'

14

We walked across the hot courtyard and through the arch towards the river. Giles clapped a hand on my shoulder and immediately let it drop again.

'Sorry I left you alone,' he said. 'But I had to pop out to . . . well, to tell someone about you before they meet you, if you see what I mean. It would have been rather a shock for them to just see you out of the blue.'

'Do you mean . . . are we going to meet Professor Holt?' I said.

Giles looked startled. 'No. No, nothing to do with Professor Holt. Whatever made you ask about Professor Holt?'

'Just that . . . didn't he know Nick really well? Was he the one that gave him a prize? And my mum and father knew him. They went on holiday with him.'

Giles frowned.

'I found that bit out from a postcard that Mum sent you,' I said. 'I'm sorry, shouldn't I have read it? It was in the album.'

He nodded. 'Yes, of course you should have read it—I gave you the album. But Professor Holt is away from Cambridge at the moment, and in any case, I suppose I knew Nick better than anyone, apart from Becky.'

'His girlfriend!' I cried.

Giles grinned. 'The album again.'

'Yes. She was really pretty,' I said.

'Ah,' said Giles, dragging a hand through his fringe.

'Yes, well, she still is. And she's . . . well, Becky and I are married. To each other. She's looking forward to meeting you. There she is!'

He was waving at someone underneath a willow on the far bank of the river. She was flapping out a rug to spread on the grass and didn't notice us. We crossed a bridge and Giles pushed aside the curtain of willow. The woman swung round to face us.

'Hi,' said Giles.

But it was me she was looking at.

Her face was strained. She flicked back her short, dark hair, then smiled and held out her hand. 'Hello, Dominic. I'm Becky.'

'Hi,' I said.

She held my hand in both hers and the smile that had been only on her lips spread to her eyes. She looked at Giles, then back to me.

'Isn't this strange?' she said. 'Strange for all of us. Giles says you've only just found out about Nick.'

'My parents never told me,' I said.

She was even prettier in real life, even though she was older now, hair shorter, face more serious. Her eyes hadn't changed, though. She'd still got my hand, and I realized that I'd started to tremble. She squeezed and let go.

'Sit down,' she said, as she knelt beside a picnic hamper and started unloading it. 'How are your parents nowadays?' she asked.

'Fine, thanks,' I said. Well, I could hardly tell the truth.

'I had a wonderful holiday with them once,' said Becky. 'Your grandad took us flying. Are your grandparents still alive?'

'Gran died just before we came back to England, when I was about nine or ten,' I said. 'We never visited this country much, so I don't remember her very well. But I've still got Pops.'

'Nick called him Pops too!' she cried. 'How is he?'

I explained as well as I could about Pops's funny state of mind. The doctors weren't sure it was Alzheimer's. They didn't really know what it was. He was just old and confused, they said.

'But he's got me,' I said. 'And Margi next door. We won't let them put him into a Retirement Unit.'

Becky and Giles smiled at each other.

'Nick would be pleased to hear that,' he said. 'He loved his grandfather very much.'

Becky handed me a plate. 'Tuck in,' she said. 'What else can we tell you about Nick?'

'Everything, please,' I said. I was starving hungry. I tucked in, spooning greedily through the pasta and piling my plate with salads.

'Well,' said Giles, 'he was a lousy cook.'

'Wasn't he just,' laughed Becky. 'He had this habit of popping round to my flat to borrow something just as I was cooking my supper. He'd say, "No, no, don't let me interrupt you, doesn't that smell good?" all in one breath. And then, one day he turned up and said he was taking me out. Not *asking* me out, you understand, just *telling* me we were going to a concert.'

'He couldn't say his alphabet right through without faltering,' said Giles.

'Like me!' I cried.

'And he always got top marks for all the exams.'

'Not like me!' I cried.

'He loved singing!'

'Like Mum!' And then I remembered something. 'Did he sing here?'

'Yes—as a matter of fact we used to sing at King's Chapel,' said Becky.

'Is that the building opposite the outfitters?' I asked.

'Yes, why?' she said.

70

'Oh, nothing,' I said. 'Carry on.'

But it wasn't nothing. It was a connection. And I'd felt it without even knowing he loved to sing.

'He sold his car to raise money for a vaccination project in Africa,' said Giles, 'and persuaded twenty other students to do the same. That was in the days when anyone was allowed to have a private car, of course.'

'He was a great campaigner,' said Becky. 'Loved going on marches and writing countless protest letters to just about everybody.'

'Or, alternatively, you could just say that he was stroppy,' grinned Giles.

A sudden silence. A pair of swans slid past on the still green river. Feelings were tugging against each other in my chest. I'd never be able to live up to this perfect son my parents had lost, this wonderful guy with his wonderful life.

'So what are your passions, Dominic?' asked Becky. 'What do you want to do?'

'Well, I'm no good at sciences, and I don't reckon I could persuade people to do things like Nick could,' I said.

I felt her eyes on me. 'That's not what I asked,' she said.

I managed to meet those gorgeous brown eyes and grin back at her.

'I like art,' I said. 'I'd like to do an art degree and . . . just hang out and paint, I suppose.'

Giles was twiddling a bread roll into crumbs. He looked up as I trailed off.

'I can't speak for Nick,' he said, 'but the thing is, I think he'd have hated to feel that you were in his shadow. He'd want you to get out there and grab life and be happy, don't you think, Becks?'

'Of course he would!'

'Well, maybe I'll come here to study,' I said. 'I've bought the uniform, so I'll have to come.'

'Uniform?' smiled Becky.

'Look!' I wriggled out of my T-shirt and turned away to rummage in my rucksack. I found one of my new sports shirts and put it on, then swung round to face them again.

'How's that?' I asked.

I hadn't expected a round of applause. But neither had I expected the reaction I got. There was blank white shock on both their faces—as if they'd seen something really terrifying.

'What's the matter?' I said.

Becky struggled to her feet and ran—a staggering run, away down the river bank.

'What's wrong?' I looked at Giles. He seemed stricken, unable to speak.

Becky had reached a bridge further down and crossed it, her dark head bobbing out of sight.

'Giles?' I turned to him again and panic surged as I saw his taut face, his clenched fists. 'What have I done? Please!'

15

'It was the birthmark,' said Giles.

I felt myself blush. I never thought about the birthmark nowadays, but people had always gawped at it when I was little. I suppose if you just glanced at it you'd think I'd been beaten or something because it's a long slash, as if someone's spilt purple-red dye, from between my shoulder blades almost to my waist. Perhaps Becky thought I'd been beaten.

'It was a shock,' said Giles, 'because Nick had a birthmark too. I suppose it brought it all back for Becky . . . '

I didn't understand. I couldn't read Giles's expression. He looked as if his mind was far away from us both. Then he snapped on a smile.

'Anyway . . . look . . . perhaps you'd like to see something of Cambridge before you leave?'

In other words, it was time for me to go. I didn't want to stay, anyway. I suddenly felt like a trespasser.

'You need to talk this out with your parents,' said Giles.

I nodded. 'I'd better get a train.'

I stared at the deserted picnic. My father wouldn't exactly be in the mood for a chat when I got back. For the first time since I'd left, I imagined what would be going on at home. My father would have gone berserk, blaming Mum for everything. And he'd be furious with me for running away.

'Don't give yourself a hard time over all this,' said Giles. 'You did the right thing coming here; but the thing is, you must live your life, that's what's important now. Believe in yourself and don't let your father . . . don't let him dictate what you should be.'

He turned away as if it hurt him to look at me.

'I'll try,' I said.

'Good man.'

'Will you say to Becky that I'm sorry I upset her?'

'It wasn't your fault,' said Giles. 'None of this is your fault, and you must always remember that. But yes, of course I'll talk to her.'

I nodded. I looked out over the river to the old buildings resting in the sun. I knew I'd never come to university here. It was a beautiful place, but it was Nick's place, not mine.

Giles and I strolled through the narrow lanes towards the station. Giles was doing his best to be chatty and point out interesting buildings. But all I could see was Becky running away from me. A few days ago I'd been a normal person and now suddenly people kept bursting into tears on me. But Giles was right. It wasn't my fault. And when I got home, I was going to tell my father that.

We had just turned into a narrow lane that ran past the side of the university outfitters, Giles chattering on about various King Henrys and which colleges they'd had built, when a woman's voice called out his name behind us. I turned, hoping it would be Becky.

It was a slim, blonde woman about Becky's age, expensively dressed. It wasn't until I heard her voice that I remembered where I'd seen her before. It was the stroppy cow who had demanded entrance to the library yesterday.

'Giles! Just the person! How lucky to see you!' she cried in a gushy voice.

She ran the few paces to join us, shaking back her short, perfectly cut hair and putting a hand on Giles's arm as she arrived.

Giles didn't look as if he felt lucky. In fact, he looked

terrified. He shifted to stand in front of me as her bright eyes and bright smile bounced between us.

'Leanne! Hello . . . ' he said.

'I've been meaning to look Becky up,' she continued. 'I'm here to cover the medical conference. We must go out for a drink. How are you fixed over the next few days? Tell Becky she must. There's a heck of a workload and I'll need to unwind.'

'Well, yes. That would be nice,' said Giles.

'How long is it since we all saw each other?' she asked, her eyes moving from him to rest on me.

'Long time,' said Giles. 'Look, Leanne, it's lovely to see you, but we've got to rush. Appointment to keep. Give us a call and we'll get together.'

He almost fell off the pavement as he grabbed my arm and we started walking off down the lane.

'Who *is* that?' I asked.

I looked back to see her staring, looking puzzled.

'Oh, no one. Old friend of Becky's. She's rather a pain.'

He glanced back and then relaxed his grip on my arm.

'Yeah, I know she is,' I said.

'What?' He looked really frightened.

'I saw her at the library yesterday,' I explained. 'She was kicking up a fuss, being really snotty to the receptionist because her card had expired.'

'Did she see you?'

'I shouldn't think so, why?'

'Are you sure?'

'Pretty sure. Why?'

'Nothing . . . it's nothing. Look, we'll get you on the next train home, yes? Then you can have a chat with your parents.'

'OK,' I said, and let myself be almost jogged along through the narrow lanes.

At the station, we found that there was a train due in ten minutes.

'Got a ticket?' asked Giles.

'Yeah.'

'Got a good book? Or a magazine or something? There's a kiosk . . . '

'I'm all right,' I said.

'Well, um . . . ' He tugged a hand through his fringe. 'Give my regards to your parents.'

I couldn't stand much more, so I said I had to go for a pee. 'And then it'll be time for the train,' I said. 'So you go.'

Suddenly he was rooting about for his wallet. He took a card and shoved it at me.

'Here are my numbers,' he said. 'If ever you need me, just call. I need you to promise . . . *promise* you won't come back here without letting me know.'

I smiled and nodded.

'No, I really mean it, Nick. Let me know. Come to me first.'

'I will, promise,' I said.

'Good luck, mate.' He lurched towards me and hugged me so hard he almost winded me. Then he spun round and hurried away. I don't think he even noticed that he'd called me Nick.

There were only a few minutes left. A train must have just come in, because people were streaming from the platform entrance. I started off, against the crowd, towards the platform.

And then I saw my father.

He was heading directly towards me but he hadn't seen me. I turned and jostled along with the crowd, out of the booking hall and into the baking sunshine. I dived towards the nearest cover, which happened to be a postbox, and leaned against the hot iron, breathless with panic. I'd seen the expression on his face. Icy cold, determined. But how had he found out? I realized almost immediately. The Jiddy card data would have told him where I'd gone. But it would also have told him I'd got a return ticket. Why the hell hadn't he just waited for me to come home?

I huddled behind the box, praying that he wouldn't come my way.

But there was someone else walking towards me, out of the sun so that she was just a blur of light colour like a ghost or an angel. As she came closer, I saw that she'd lost the jacket of her suit and now wore a white blouse above the lilac skirt. She lifted a hand to smooth her hair.

'Mr Gordon?' she asked.

I hesitated. 'My name's Dominic,' I said.

She stared at me, then held out a hand for me to shake. I took it and felt the coolness of her palm as she squeezed.

'I recognized you the instant I saw you. Why have you come to Cambridge?'

At the very edge of my vision, I could see my father at the station entrance. He was scanning the forecourt, looking for a taxi.

'I was . . . my brother used to be a student . . . ' I said.

She nodded and raised her hand. A private car with tinted glass slid forwards and she opened the back door.

'Come with me and we'll have a chat. I was your brother's tutor. Professor Holt. It's good to meet you.'

And now my father was looking in our direction, looking to see if this car was a taxi.

I ducked into the leather interior of the car. Professor Holt slipped in beside me and the driver pulled away before she'd even shut the door.

16

As we rolled forwards past the entrance to the station, my father glared into the car with a look that burned straight into me and stopped my breath. Then he looked away. I slumped back against the seat, smiling inside. Even *he* couldn't see through tinted glass. The car gathered speed. Professor Holt slid a hand towards me across the cool leather. Close to, you could see she was older than she seemed from a distance. There were creases around her eyes and mouth, threads of silver in the blonde. But she was very beautiful. All her colours were cool pastel except her eyes, which were the most fantastic colour of honey-hazel.

'I see you've got a Grenville Hall shirt,' she said.

'Yes,' I said. 'It was my brother's college.' And then I felt stupid because, of course, she would know that. She'd probably think I was an idiot compared to him, anyway.

'What have your parents told you about Nick?' she asked.

'Nothing,' I said. 'They wanted to keep him a secret.' As soon as I said this, my face began to burn. I hadn't meant to let her know so much.

'They didn't tell you that you had a brother?' she said. 'So when did you make this discovery?'

'Couple of days ago.'

'How?'

Again I felt hot under the cool gaze of those clever eyes. She had a way of looking and listening so intently that you felt you were under a microscope.

78

'I found some photos in my grandfather's loft. It was obvious he was my brother. We look so alike.'

She explored my face again in detail, like a bee on a flower. 'Yes,' she said. 'So you've run away from home?'

I nodded and remembered that she'd seen me arrive on my own. She'd been watching me ever since—it couldn't have been coincidence that I'd kept seeing her. How stupid I'd been! In the panic to get away from my father, I hadn't stopped to think, but now I did. And I couldn't think of one good reason why she'd be interested in me unless it was to compare me to Nick.

'Have you met Dr Nickalls?' she asked.

'Yes.'

'Anybody else?'

'Only his wife, Becky,' I said.

'Hmm.' She nodded.

I looked away, embarrassed at being examined, desperately trying to think of a way of getting away from her without being rude. I remembered something else. Giles had told me Professor Holt was away from Cambridge. He also hadn't corrected me when I'd assumed Professor Holt was a man.

'Professor Holt,' I said, 'I've just remembered that I said I'd meet Dr Nickalls. So I won't have time to go anywhere. I'm sorry, could you drop me off?'

A phone rang and she leaned down to fish it out of a briefcase.

'Hello, Debbie.' She glanced across at me as she listened. 'One moment.'

She covered the mouthpiece and, with a tiny smile creasing the sides of her mouth, said, 'It looks as though your father has tracked you down. He's here in Cambridge and he's asking to see me.'

'Why?' I said.

She shrugged. 'Shall we go and meet him?'

'No!'

I thought I saw a trace of a smile as she turned back to the phone and said, 'No, Debbie. Say I'm out of the country. And don't call again unless it's an emergency.' She snapped the phone shut and looked at me.

'We'll have a nice afternoon together, just the two of us. I want you to see the Foundation where Nick studied. And then perhaps you'll come home for a bite of supper and I'll get my pilot to take you home. Where do you live?'

'Surrey, but you needn't . . . '

'No problem.'

But there was a problem. I wondered why she was siding with me against my father.

'Didn't you use to be friends with my parents?' I asked.

This seemed to surprise her.

'Well, I'd met them through Nick, of course.' She smiled.

'And you went on holiday together. To the Cayman Islands?'

Definite surprise now, but she hid it well.

'And from where did you glean that piece of information?' she asked.

'There was a postcard from my mother to Dr Nickalls,' I said. 'She said you'd been really good to them after Nick died and that you all went to the Cayman Islands together.'

She nodded. 'We did. It was a very difficult time for your parents. I felt they needed a break.'

'That's what Mum said in the postcard.'

She turned to look out of the window. I didn't know what to think. She wasn't going to turn me in to my father or tell me I shouldn't have run away or any of that stuff. And if Mum had been friends with her, then she must be all right.

80

'Look,' she said, pointing out of the window, 'here we are.'

I could see glimpses of a white building beyond trees as we flashed past them. Suddenly the trees cleared and we swung into a wide gravel driveway leading towards what looked like a white marble palace. A slab, engraved with gold, at the entrance to the drive, said 'The Holt Foundation'.

'It's named after you,' I said, and immediately went red again. There was something about her that made me keep saying stupid things. I was glad she didn't turn to look at me. She seemed to be admiring her building.

'It bears my name but it's really an international research centre,' she said. 'We have top scientists from all over the world working here.'

The car stopped at the foot of a wide sweep of steps.

'And Nick worked here?' I said.

'Yes. His year was the first to use the new laboratories. It might interest you.'

'What did they do, in the laboratories?'

'Oh, all sorts of things. Nick was studying life sciences.'

We walked up the steps that, I was amazed to see, were actually made of marble, into a huge foyer with glass security doors leading off it. Halfway up the wall opposite the entrance was a hologram platform and underneath it was written 'Professor Imogen Holt' in gold lettering.

'Can I play it?' I asked.

'Of course.'

I touched the panel under the inscription and stood back as the hologram burst into life on the platform. It showed the marble steps that we had just climbed. Professor Holt, a little younger than she was now, was coming down them, followed by a bunch of people, some of them in white coats. In the foreground were a whole load of old-fashioned microphones and cameras. She walked up to them and began talking, her voice slightly shaky.

'We are very proud and happy to give here today, news of a long-awaited breakthrough in medical science. Our extensive trials on live patients are concluded and we can now state unequivocally that we have the techniques to re-grow nerve tissue. This means that in paraplegic patients and others suffering nerve damage, we can produce a return to normal mobility. I am delighted to announce that we have had one hundred per cent success in cases treated thus far.'

She smiled at the cameras and gestured for three people to walk forward. There was a murmur of excitement from the invisible crowd in front of her as the two men and a woman stepped up to join her at the microphone. There was a huge roar of cheering, clapping, and whistles as the woman began to speak. I recognized her. She was a famous American actress.

The actress finished her speech thanking Professor Holt for making her walk again, and then the hologram vanished. I spun round to Imogen, a memory from way back springing into life just as the hologram had.

'I remember that day! I've seen it before! I was at junior school in the States and we were all given the afternoon off to have a huge party. My best friend ate too much and was sick!'

She laughed for the first time, the smooth white skin at the sides of her mouth rippling into creases. 'And I thought I'd dedicated my life to curing sickness!'

I looked away. The most famous doctor in the world. I should have known who she was! I *had* seen her before!

'Come on.' She turned to one of the glass security doors. 'I want to show you what I hope will be our next big announcement.'

I followed her down corridors into the marble heart of

the building. We passed no one and for a long time the only sound was the clicking of her heels and the squeak of my shoes. We reached a lift and she put her hand into a scanner. The doors slid open.

'You know,' she said as the doors closed on us, 'in many ways, Nick was part of the research that led to that area of treatment. He had a way of finding new questions, or framing old questions differently so that you could see things in a fresh way. He had a real gift for original, creative thought. All great people have that gift—scientists, philosophers, composers, artists . . .'

'Artists?' I was surprised.

'Of course,' she said. 'Look at—I don't know . . .'

'Picasso,' I interrupted. 'He saw the world in a fresh way.'

'In just the same way as, say, Galileo or Einstein.'

'Or Leonardo da Vinci!' I said. 'He had a brain the size of a planet!'

'Yes, but it's not only brain, is it?—or intellect, I suppose you'd call it—it's intellect plus intuition plus intense curiosity, technical aptitude, instinct . . . so many things. There's a complex alchemy in the creative mind which turns the ordinary into the extraordinary—pushes on our understanding of the world.'

We were out of the lift and now she was opening a door, hitting a light switch, leading the way into what looked like a laboratory. We must be way underground.

'Are those scanners?' I asked, looking at the grim machines at the end of the room. One of them looked as if you had to lie inside a sort of giant pipe.

'Yes, we're using them for our current project.'

She hit a switch on a light board. There were three or four scans clipped to the board.

'Have a look at these,' she said.

'Oh no, I'm no good at scientific things.'

83

'Really? You mean—not interested, or really no good at it?'

'I . . . I don't know. There are just things I can't understand,' I said.

'Understanding begins with good observation skills,' she said. 'Just look and tell me what you see. Want an orange juice?'

'Yes—thanks.'

I stared in bewilderment at the scans. It seemed to me that they were just four pictures of a sort of white island in a black sea. I looked more closely. The first island was huge compared to the other three. The second scan showed the island getting smaller. And then I saw a shape behind the island, the landscape in which it was set. There were lines that looked like ribs and I guessed that I was looking at someone's chest. Once I had made the guess, the pictures began to make more sense.

'What do you deduce?' asked Professor Holt, handing me some juice. I gulped at it, soon draining the glass.

'It could be someone's chest. Is the white patch . . . is it cancer?' I asked.

She drew up the stool next to mine. 'Right first time. This is the final phase of our cancer treatment research. The patient has advanced lung cancer, as you see from the first scan. On the second scan, you can see that the cancer is receding. On the third, things are looking better still, and on the fourth . . . '

'You've cured it!'

'Not quite, but we think we'll soon be there. I've got a really crack team working on this—the best from all over the world. We think we've succeeded in promoting the growth of new lung cells in such a way that the cancer can't attack them again. It's a step on from the re-growing of nerve cells that we pioneered with the paraplegic patients.'

84

'Wow! I can see why Nick was really into this sort of stuff!'

'Yet you say you're no good at it?' She looked puzzled.

'It's the maths and the formulae and stuff I can't do. My father says I'm not applying my brain properly.'

I felt her eyes on me as I looked at the scans again. I wanted to understand more, I wanted to prove that I could apply my brain, but my eyes wouldn't focus properly. I blinked. I suddenly felt very tired.

'I'm sorry, Professor Holt,' I said, 'but I feel really sleepy.'

My voice sounded loud inside my own head, but hers sounded very far away.

'Call me Imogen, please. Why don't you hop up on the couch and have a little snooze, then.'

17

When I woke, it felt as if no time had passed at all. I was still on the couch where Professor Holt had put me and I could see her sitting, with her back to me, in front of the light board. She was studying some more scans, this time of somebody's brain.

'Sorry—I fell asleep,' I said.

She switched off the light board as she turned to me.

'Only to be expected. You've had a tough time lately. Rest a few minutes, and when you feel up to it, we'll go home.'

I lay down again and watched her pack up her work. She gathered up some papers, unclipped the scans and took it all through to a little room, where she unlocked a wall safe.

'I have a swimming-pool,' she called, as she bundled her things into the safe. 'Do you enjoy swimming?'

'Yes, I do. But—'

'Good.'

'Professor Holt?' There was something I needed to know, and she was the only one I could ask.

'Call me Imogen, won't you?' She came to sit on the couch.

'Where is Nick now?'

A look of pain flitted across her face.

'Oh, I don't mean is he in Heaven, or any of that stuff,' I said. 'I mean—I don't even know where they had the funeral.'

'He was cremated. Here in Cambridge.'

'Is there anything I can . . . you know, go and look at?'

'Isn't that a bit morbid?' she said, a slight sharpness in her voice.

I was annoyed. She had, after all, wanted to talk to me about Nick and show me things.

'I hadn't thought of it like that,' I said. I'd ask Giles, if she didn't want to talk about it.

'Ready to go?' She picked up her briefcase.

I still felt a bit muzzy but I didn't like to say so. I'd be better in the open air, anyway. I got down off the couch, and we set off up through the silent building.

We hadn't driven far when she asked the chauffeur to pull over and she got out of the car and opened my door.

'Follow me,' she said. 'There's something you'll want to see.'

I followed her across a green towards the river. From here you could see the back of Grenville Hall. There was a copse of trees and Professor Holt stopped beside one of them. It wasn't very big. A young oak. She bent down and pulled some grass away from a plaque.

'Here,' she said. 'It's where they buried his ashes.'

'And planted a tree for him?' I said.

She nodded.

I bent to read the plaque.

DOMINIC MICHAEL GORDON
1 MARCH 1980–19 FEBRUARY 2001
'Ever the best of friends'

'Did Giles put this here?' I asked.

When she didn't answer, I looked up and caught her staring at me in a strange, distracted way that seemed to wipe all the life out of her face. She looked away.

'Yes.'

87

She turned and strode off towards the car. I looked at the bright leaves of Nick's tree with their crinkled edges. A great idea, to plant a tree. Just the sort of thing that a best mate would do.

As we drove out of Cambridge, Professor Holt was quiet, staring out of the window, but as we reached the flat, bright countryside, she turned and said, 'So tell me all about you. Big exams next year, yes?'

I didn't remember telling her my age, but I supposed it was a reasonable guess that I'd be doing exams soon. I seemed to have spent most of my life doing them. I nodded. 'Yeah.'

'Which are your best subjects?'

'Art,' I said.

'And?'

'Just Art, really,' I said. I could see where this was leading.

'Hmm,' she said. 'Then you must draw something for me. But first, a swim.'

Later, she sat at the side of the pool and watched as I hurtled down the chute, hit the shimmering blue water and swam down towards the bright mosaic at the bottom.

'Are those trunks OK?' she called out as I surfaced.

'They're fine—thanks.'

She'd lent me a pair of trunks and after I'd drawn the cord as tight as it would go they just about stayed up. They belonged to her husband, who was an actor. She'd proudly shown me their wedding picture, taken last year. He was very good-looking, quite a bit younger than her. He was away for the weekend, auditioning for a part in a film.

She watched as I swam around for a while. Then I came to the side of the pool, so thirsty that I downed glass after glass of mineral water, but she didn't seem to mind.

'Draw me a picture of the house,' she said.

I looked at the old Tudor building with its mass of

different rooflines, some of them sagging with mossy old tiles, and a timber frame which bulged out in places so that it looked as if it was about to collapse. The whole thing was a real challenge to perspective.

'I'll try,' I said.

'I'll see if I can find some paper and things,' she said.

She jumped up and headed for the house, leaping over the hot bricks of the courtyard in her bare feet. By the time she'd got back I'd dried myself and pulled my shirt on over the trunks. I pinched the umbrella from the recliner and repositioned the garden table so that I got the best view of the house.

'Here you are, Picasso.' She smiled.

She'd brought paper and coloured pencils and a box of watercolour paints and some brushes.

'I used to keep this stuff for when my nieces and nephews came to stay,' she said. 'It's pretty ancient, I'm afraid.'

'It doesn't matter, these paints are really good,' I said.

I set it all up, with a large sheet of paper stretched over a board resting on the garden table.

'I'll be pottering in the kitchen,' she said.

I nodded, desperate to get going. The shadows of evening were just beginning to bleed out from the house and there was an amazing light in the sky, the East Anglian sky that so many artists had loved. I could see why. There was so much more sky than anything else because the land was so flat, and it seemed to cast a strange light on everything, turning the ordinary into the extraordinary—alchemy, as Imogen would say. I hoped I could do it justice.

Much later, as the light was beginning to fade, she came out with food and some wax torches. She stuck the torches in the ground and lit them.

'May I see?' she asked.

It's horrible, that moment when you hand your work over to someone else. Hope and fear, faith and doubt are all in a muddy mix like the brushwater. Something is stubborn inside you, and something cowers. And even if someone says it's good, you don't dare believe them.

'This is good,' she said. 'Really good!'

'D'you think so?'

She took the painting and held it under one of the torches.

'This thing you've done with the light,' she said. 'How did you do that? It's so right, you've got it exactly!'

I saw that she was really interested, she really understood. We ate and talked.

'The thing is,' I said, 'I don't just want to be good at painting, that's not what it's about. It's about exploring something—seeing where it takes you, how far you can go, you know?'

I looked up and caught her watching me with a warmer, deeper sort of watching than before. She nodded. 'I know exactly what you mean. I feel the same as a scientist.'

'My father's against it,' I said. 'I think he wishes I was like Nick.'

'But you *are* like Nick!' she cried. 'You have an exceptional talent! Your technical ability alone is extraordinary, but your interpretation of what you see—that's what's truly fascinating.'

We stared at each other across the torchlight.

'You have to follow your hunger for something, Dominic, and you've got a hunger for this, just as Nick had a hunger for exploring science. It's the same thing!'

She swiped back her hair, which had fallen loose.

'You need an ally,' she said.

We grinned at each other for a split second and then her eyes moved away from me. There was a tiny sound buzzing somewhere in the hot night. An engine noise. It came closer and suddenly there was a light sweeping across the darkening water of the pool, then a scrunching of gravel and the dying throb of a motorbike being turned off.

Imogen stood up.

'It's Simeon,' she said, 'my husband. I wasn't expecting him back. I hope this doesn't mean the audition was a disaster!'

18

She ran to meet him. He took off his helmet and wrapped her up in a hug.

I fiddled around, tidying plates, while they stood in the darkness talking. I wondered what I should do with my picture. I wanted her to have it. I swirled a dramatic signature in the bottom right hand corner.

'What's this?' said a deep, laughing voice behind me. 'I can't leave my wife on her own for five minutes!'

I swung round. He had the sort of face you think you must have seen in a film, but I hadn't seen him before, apart from in their wedding photo. It was just that I knew the type. Strong, good-looking, with a confident way of looking directly at you. He held out his hand.

'Hello, Dominic. So you think you might like to come to Cambridge to study?'

The squeeze of his handshake hurt.

'I was just telling Simeon that your parents are old friends,' said Imogen.

'Yes,' I said, not knowing which statement I was supposed to answer.

'So—who are your parents?' he asked, his eyes holding my face.

'Oh, Carla and Michael. You've never met them,' said Imogen.

Simeon took off his gloves and unzipped his leather jacket. 'Well, Dominic,' he said, 'tomorrow you must get out and about and really see the place. I'll take you on the bike. Can you ride a motorbike? Which college was it you're after?'

Imogen laughed. 'Don't mind my husband, Dominic. He does love to organize people!'

'Don't often get to take anyone on the bike,' said Simeon, pulling a long face. 'Immie won't go near it, will you, darling?'

'Because you drive like a maniac! Let's go in and have some coffee,' said Imogen.

In the huge, flagstoned kitchen, I tried to make myself useful with washing-up, but there was a dishwasher. I sat at the table and watched them load the machine and make coffee. I'd never seen two people like this before. The way she bent her head towards him, the way he rested a hand on her waist. Just the way they looked at each other.

They came to the table with a coffee tray.

'Could do with a drink, really, after the day I've had,' said Simeon.

'Have one, then,' said Imogen.

He went to a cupboard and got out a bottle of whisky.

'Simeon isn't sure yet whether he got the part. It was for a film,' said Imogen.

'Your face has to fit what they're looking for. It was probably all a waste of time,' he said. He took a swig of whisky and came to sit close to me, looking at me again with a directness that made me shift slightly in my seat. 'So—you must be a clever young fellow if you're in the running to study with my wife!'

'Oh, I'm not in the running to study with her,' I said.

'He is, however, a very clever young fellow,' said Imogen. 'He's painted me a wonderful picture of the house. You can keep the paints, Dominic.'

She pushed the box towards me.

'Oh, no. They're . . . well, they're expensive,' I said.

93

'You're worth it,' she smiled. 'Anyway, they'll only go to waste here.'

'OK. Thanks very much.'

She slid one hand across the table to squeeze Simeon's hand. With the other, she patted mine. I sipped at my coffee, trying to finish it quickly, but it was hot.

She looked at me. 'I bet you're tired,' she said. 'Shall I show you your room?'

I nodded. 'I've left the picture over there. I've signed it, too, if you really want to keep it.'

'Thank you. I shall treasure it always,' she said.

I felt my face go red and I turned away from her to pack the box of paints away in my rucksack. Simeon got up and went to pick up the picture, which I'd leaned against the wall. He turned it over to look at it as we left the room.

I followed Imogen through a sitting room in the middle of the house. It had a gallery running round it at first-floor height, with a creaky staircase leading up to it. There were loads of doors leading off the gallery and she showed me into a room with a huge four-poster bed.

'There are towels in the cupboard,' she said. 'However, I'm afraid the Tudors didn't run to en-suite bathrooms. Follow me!'

We went out onto the gallery again and a few doors further down there was a bathroom.

'I meant what I said about the picture,' she said. 'I'm going to get it framed. I shall treasure it always. Sleep well.'

And before I knew she was going to do it, she brushed her hand against my face, then turned quickly to walk back down the gallery.

I did sleep well for a while. But the thirst that had begun after we left the Foundation was still there. It woke me suddenly in the pitch dark of the unfamiliar room. At first I couldn't remember where I was. Then the last few days washed back over me and I remembered the train, Zita, the outfitters shop, Bulldog-face, Giles, Becky, Imogen. I couldn't believe that I'd dared to run away and now I was lying in this huge bed in a stranger's house and nobody knew where I was. Tomorrow I'd have to go home, but somehow meeting Imogen had helped—to have someone that clever who believed in me, who seemed to understand why I wanted to be an artist. I snuggled deeper into the bed, feeling peaceful and happy. But it was no good, I'd still have to get a drink. The thirst was killing me.

I turned on the bedside lamp and slipped out of bed. Very carefully, I opened the creaky old door. I had no idea what time it was and I didn't want to wake Imogen and Simeon if they were asleep. But there was light coming up from the living room, so they must still be up. I was about to head off down the gallery to the bathroom when I heard a sort of strangled shout from the room below. It was Simeon's voice.

'God!' he said. Just that.

I waited, breathing in the smell of dry, ages-old wood from the beams around me. And then Simeon went on.

'God, if I'd known when I came back tonight that *that boy* . . . that it was *him*! Immie, you're just not thinking about what could happen! Now, of all times! Why didn't you leave the boy alone? Just walk away?'

'I couldn't. Not once I'd seen him.'

'But you told me the deal was you'd have no contact with him. Ever. That's what the Gordons wanted.'

'I couldn't walk away. I *know* it was wrong!'

'It's not just wrong, Immie, it's dangerous! If anyone makes a connection between you and him . . . '

'They won't. There's no proof.'

'Oh, come *on*! A simple DNA test would do it.'

'It's *not* that simple!'

95

There was a silence, then Simeon said, 'Is there anyone else who knows about him? Who else has he seen?'

'He went to see Giles Nickalls today. There'd be no reason for Giles to know anything, though.'

'Well, we'd better just pray that the Wishart investigation doesn't come anywhere near you. Because if Wishart mentions your name . . .'

Another silence. Then I heard him get up. I heard the stifled anger in his next words. 'I'd do *anything* to protect you, Immie. I mean it! Why now, for God's sake? Why did your precious baby have to turn up *now*?'

'DON'T call him that!'

'Well, that's what he is, isn't he? He's *your baby* . . .'

'You BASTARD! I wish I'd never told you about him!'

A door slammed somewhere.

Whoever it was that was left began to sob.

19

I felt an icy sweat all over me and a sickening sense of panic. It couldn't be true. Imogen, my mother.

I stood listening to the sobs coming from the room below as the second wave hit me. That was the sickness feeling, the impossibility of the idea that Mum wasn't my mum. If she wasn't my mum, then my whole life had a huge great lie hiding behind it. To even think of her not being my real mother was like losing her—I'd lost the person I thought she was. And what about my father? It was all so impossible. And then it dawned on me that it wasn't impossible. My father had known Imogen before I was born. Did I look like Imogen? Another wave of panic. I did—a bit. And we both had blonde hair.

The sobbing below stopped and I saw Simeon walk out of the room. Somewhere a door closed and the house fell silent. Anger surged inside me and I ran back to my room and got dressed. They were going to tell me. I'd make them tell me.

I clattered down the old wooden staircase and ran through the galleried room, through the kitchen, and out into the hot, heavy darkness. Before I'd rounded the side of the house I could hear them in the courtyard ahead of me. I stopped, hiding behind some sort of climbing plant that was giving off a sickly scent. I'd get more truth by overhearing than by asking. I'd learnt that much at least.

Simeon's voice had a desperate, shaken sort of anger.

'You've got to let him go!' he was saying. 'It's the best thing for all of us—including him. I'm not going to let you get hurt over this, Immie. There's no way I'll let that happen!'

'I know, I know,' she said. She sounded wrung-out, defeated.

'I'm only trying to protect you, darling,' he said. 'I'm sorry . . .'

Like hell he was. He was the one who wanted me off the scene, wasn't he?

'I just feel that it's better for him to know the truth,' she said.

'No, Immie!' His voice rose almost to a shout. 'For God's sake, listen to me! It's too much of a risk for you. What do you think would happen if he found out the truth now? You've *got* to forget about him. That's the price you have to pay for what you did.'

'He's a great kid, isn't he?' she said. 'You know, fifteen years ago I had no doubts about what I was doing. I just got on with it. Didn't allow myself to feel anything. But seeing him now, all these years later—well, he's *made* me feel. And think. It's quite remarkable how—'

'I'll tell you what's remarkable—that the little beggar chooses to turn up *now*,' said Simeon bitterly.

'Don't be angry with him, darling. This is all *my* fault, not his,' she sighed.

They fell silent and I edged forwards, my heart kicking at my chest. I could see them clearly. Some light from the house was picking up a gentle ripple on the pool and reflecting a dancing pattern on her skirt. Simeon was rocking her in his arms. I wanted to run out and ask her why she had given me away, why she hadn't felt anything. But I couldn't move.

'You're right,' she said at last, 'I should never have picked him up—or brought him here. I'll send him home tomorrow.'

'It's the best thing,' he said, his voice calmer now.

'There'll be no reason for me to see him ever again, and I'm sure the Gordons wouldn't want that anyway.'

'Come and have a drink,' he said.

She made a weak laughing sound. 'It's three o'clock in the morning!'

'OK, just bed then,' he said.

As they came towards me round the side of the house, my heart raced so much that I could hardly breathe. They had their arms round each other, hugged together, walking slowly. I tried to think of what I was going to say. They would look up any moment and see me and I had to be ready.

But they didn't see me. And I didn't speak. They walked past me, only feet away in the darkness, and through the kitchen door. Still I couldn't speak, my voice choked up in my throat. They closed the door behind them.

What was there to say, anyway? She didn't want me. She wasn't going to make life difficult for herself. She picked me up because she was curious to see how I'd turned out, but she didn't want me. As I stood, numb and stupid, wondering what to do next, the lights in the house went off, one by one.

And then a vicious energy took hold of me and I set off walking fast, faster and faster, breaking into a stumbling run. I didn't know where I was going, I just knew I couldn't stay where I was. Had to keep moving, running away from the nightmare I had blundered into. They should have told me. I ran on through a vast, shaved, stubble field. The pain of knowing that they had all kept the secret was tearing at my chest. I stopped in the middle of the field, wanting to scream, to get the pain out somehow. But I didn't scream. I stopped, listening to my heartbeat and my breathing and the sound of crickets in the hot darkness around me.

Away in the distance, spires and rooflines were charcoaled

against the pinkish glow of the Cambridge lights. I needed to talk to Giles. He'd tried to keep me away from Imogen. I remembered what he had said at the station. 'Come to me first. Promise me.' Go to him instead of whom? Instead of her, of course. Just what did Giles know about it all? I turned towards Cambridge and walked on.

20

Since hearing that I was Imogen's baby, I'd forgotten about my brother. But as I crunched through the prickly stubble in the middle of the night, with everything in my life collapsing around me, I thought about him. If I was Imogen's baby, so was he. My likeness to him was so strong. But was that possible? Imogen has two sons, twenty-two years apart, and hands them both over to my parents? Nobody would do that, would they? But if she hadn't done that, then what was Imogen doing in our lives? Was she our mother, or not? She must be. Otherwise, why would Simeon have said *'He's your baby!'*? But no, that was wrong. I knew it was wrong because I knew . . . I *knew* in the very centre of my being that I was Mum's son.

I strode on, thinking until I thought I would go mad, trying to crack open the secrets.

I came to the river. The dawn was coming and I sat down on the bank.

It's a strange thing, the dawn. People ought to see it more often because it's a weird mix of peaceful and exciting. It's as if everything is gathering up to make a start, like an orchestra twiddling to get the right notes before a concert. The real thing hasn't begun yet, but it's nearly here. Birds getting ready. Light pushing at the greyness. A change in the air. Things are creeping up on you, gradually sorting themselves out for a beginning.

And that's how my thoughts sorted themselves out. Gradually. Could you have two mothers? Yes. How could two mothers, Imogen and Carla, Carla and Imogen, make a

101

baby between them? Easy. One could be a surrogate, using the other's egg. But there was just one problem. You couldn't do that and get two sons who looked exactly the same. Could you? I stared across at the odd little towers and spires of the Cambridge skyline and thought about my brother. The two of us. I didn't want to think what I was beginning to think.

I turned and turned the idea in my head and every way I thought of it, it fitted. My father wanting me to be something I wasn't, my mother soaking her mind in booze to blot out the horror of what they'd done. Maybe even Pops going mad. And the more I turned the idea over, the more my heart hammered the blood round my body and my skin flushed hot and cold, as if in revulsion at itself.

I pulled my mobile out of my jeans pocket. Loads of messages from my father stacked up. No wonder. He must have been going out of his mind. With shaking hands, I unlocked the keyboard and phoned Giles.

'It's Dominic,' I told the bleary voice at the other end.

'Dominic!' Immediately the fog cleared from his voice. 'Are you OK, mate? Where are you?'

'Still in Cambridge,' I said. 'I've got to see you.'

'OK . . . but you sound bad. Are you all right?'

'No. I need to talk to you. Can you come?'

'Where are you?'

'I'll meet you at the Holt Foundation,' I said. I wanted to see that hologram one last time.

'I'm on my way.'

'OK.'

As the light began to take a hold, I wandered downstream towards the Holt Foundation. The marble was shimmering, as if the place was some sort of magical temple.

She'd taken me in there and given me a drug to make me sleep. And then she'd checked me over. And I was so stupid, so amazed by her and her cleverness and the great

102

temple to her achievements, that I'd fallen asleep without even asking why I suddenly felt drowsy.

I crossed the dewy lawns and walked up the marble steps.

I played the hologram. I played it over and over and heard again and again the famous announcement. 'I repeat—we have the technique to regenerate nerve tissue.' I looked at her beautiful face. The cleverest doctor in the world.

As the applause died away for the last time, I heard her voice again.

'Dominic.'

I spun round.

She was leaning against a marble pillar, watching me.

'What are you doing here?' I said.

'I came looking for you when I found you'd gone,' she said. She was as tense as a cat squaring up for a fight, you could sense it. 'I was just driving round, really,' she said, her voice too bright. 'I didn't know where you'd be heading. I saw the hologram from the road. Dominic, are you all right?'

'You tell me,' I said. 'You're the famous doctor.'

She came towards me, looking hard at me. She was searching for a clue. How much did I know?

'I'm sorry, Dominic. I didn't mean for you to overhear whatever it was that you overheard—that made you run away . . .'

'You're not really my mother, are you? Not exactly,' I said.

It must have been disappointing for her that I'd taken so long to work it out. Nick would have got it at once. There were more footsteps and Giles ran up towards us.

'Dominic?' he cried. And then he saw Imogen and went as pale as the marble around him. 'What's happening here?' he asked.

'No,' said Imogen, her beautiful eyes holding mine, 'I'm not your mother, Dominic.'

'Professor Holt,' snapped Giles, 'before you go any further with this, I need to speak to you in private. As a matter of extreme urgency.'

'I wish I was, but I'm not.' She smiled.

'Professor Holt, you *must* listen, *please*!' cried Giles. 'There's news from the European Courts. It came over the Net late last night. Wishart has been convicted. He could face the death penalty.'

This whatever-it-was that was so important—it got to her. She looked as though she couldn't believe it.

'Who's Wishart?' I asked.

'A doctor,' she said, frowning. 'He's been on trial in Brussels.'

'On trial for what?' I said.

'Professor Holt!' snapped Giles.

'He broke a global prohibition. A prohibition that carries the death penalty.'

She was looking at her own slim foot as it traced a circle on the white marble. 'He tried to clone a human being,' she said.

'Only tried?' I said.

'He didn't succeed.'

'Not as clever as you, then,' I said.

'No.' She threw her head up to look at me. 'I did succeed. As you know.'

'Did you do any more?' I asked. 'Or just me?'

She made the tiniest shake of her head, her eyes still holding mine.

'There are no more, Dominic. You're the only one.'

21

'**P**rofessor Holt, this is utterly irresponsible!' cried Giles. 'It's . . . it's cruel! What possible good can come from him knowing about what you did?'

'You're insulting his intelligence, Giles,' said Imogen. 'He'd have found out one day.'

'I don't see how! It's hardly the sort of thing you'd guess!' cried Giles.

'SHUT UP! SHUT UP!' I yelled.

I was sick of people fighting about me. And this fight was worse than any of the others because it meant that it really was true. I'd wanted her to tell me I'd got it wrong, but deep down I knew I hadn't. Imogen had cloned my brother to make me. I sank onto the cold floor. I looked at my fists, clenched against my knees. What did it mean? Was this his body? Were they his fists? Grown from him. How could I call myself 'me' any more?

Giles knelt beside me. I wasn't crying this time. There wasn't enough left in me for crying.

'Dominic, I'm your friend,' he said. 'And I'll do anything I can to help you. Now and always. That's a promise.'

I felt light-headed and sick. And I had the strangest feeling of everything emptying out of me so that I couldn't move or think properly. I was just someone else's experiment. Not me any more. I looked up at Imogen.

'WHY?' I cried. 'Why did you do it?'

She twisted her head away from me and sighed.

'I don't . . . Dominic, I don't think this is the right time. You're in shock . . . '

'Oh, so shall I make an appointment? When I'm not in shock? Well, I'm sorry, I don't know when that will be, so I'm asking you now. WHY DID YOU DO IT?'

The marble walls threw the strange scream of my voice back at me and then there was silence. At last she turned to look at me again.

'Because I wanted to see if it *could* be done. That's the truth.'

'"It" meaning me, one person made from another, exactly the same? So I was an experiment, something made in your laboratory! You must think you're so clever, you can make anything, control anything!'

She turned away suddenly and leant a hand against the wall next to the gold plaque bearing her name. The other hand went to her face.

'You don't know what it's done to me!' I cried.

I thought I heard a sob stab the cool air. I felt rage. How could *she* be crying? She was all right. She could do whatever she liked in her life. She was free. But I was made for a purpose—to replace Nick—and I had to live my life knowing that I was a duff copy of the original.

'I HATE you!' I yelled.

Giles moved suddenly to stand between us.

'Please,' he said quietly. 'This can't help.'

'You don't know what she did, Giles! She gave me stuff to knock me out and then she examined me! That's what she did, ask her! I'm just some sort of laboratory rat to her!'

'Yes, I examined you,' she said, turning back to me. If she had been crying, you couldn't tell now. 'I checked for the birthmark. I never saw you as a baby, you see. I was informed that you'd been safely delivered and that you were healthy. After that there was to be no more contact between us. I thought I would never see you. And then, suddenly, there you were, stepping off a train . . . ' She faltered, shrugged, rubbed a hand over her temples and then continued, her voice sharper. 'Naturally I wanted to see if the birthmark was there. It would be the only conclusive visual proof—to anyone who knew that Nick had the same mark—that you were his clone. Anything that Nick had at birth, you would have also.'

The sickness feeling came again as I heard those words, 'you were his clone'. I remembered Becky running away from that birthmark and what it meant. Nick's body, born again. I hated Imogen for her calmness. But I needed to know.

'Tell me, then,' I said, trying to control the tremble of anger. 'How? How did you make me from Nick?'

She came to sit on the marble step beside me. Not too close, but close enough. 'The process is called somatic cell nuclear transfer,' she said in a low, steady voice. 'This means that you take a somatic cell—that's any body cell other than an egg or sperm—from the donor. You then transfer this somatic cell into an unfertilized egg. This egg has had its own nucleus removed, so the somatic cell from the donor replaces the nucleus. You implant the egg back into the mother and the whole grows just like a fertilized egg, just like a normal baby.'

I was trembling so hard I could hardly control it. This was me she was talking about.

'So the donor was Nick?' I managed to say.

'Yes.'

'And the egg was Mum's?'

'Yes.'

'So where does my father fit in to all this?'

A faint smile brushed her cheek.

'Well, one way of looking at it is that he doesn't fit in much at all, except in as much as he was Nick's father and therefore, by extension, yours. It is rather a biological conundrum.'

107

'And it was his idea.'

'Yes.'

'What about Mum?'

Imogen sighed. 'Carla was too . . . She was out of her mind with grief after Nick's death. I don't know, I can't say whether she made a rational decision.'

'Oh, she wouldn't have been allowed to make a *decision*!' I yelled. 'No one makes a *decision* with my father around! And with you on his side, who could argue anyway? You're both the same! You think you can control EVERYTHING!'

Giles grabbed my arm as an electrocar scrunched onto the gravel below us. A man got out and began unloading gardening tools.

'Lovely morning, Professor Holt!' he called up the steps.

'This isn't the place to be having this discussion,' hissed Giles as the gardener headed off across the lawn.

'I suppose not,' I said bitterly. 'I'd better shut up, hadn't I? If this Wishart chap is in so much trouble for just *trying* to clone someone, then how much trouble will Professor Holt be in if anyone finds out about me?'

Imogen turned on me suddenly, her golden eyes blazing.

'Before you threaten me, think. Just think,' she said, 'what your life would be like if the world media came after you, the only clone in the world.'

'I'd make a lot of money,' I said.

'You're not fooling me, Dominic. Go back with Giles now, get some rest. I'll come and see you later.'

She stood up and strode down the steps.

'Yeah, and *you* go back to your perfect life!' I cried. 'Before your husband notices you've gone. Because if he finds out you've come running after me there'll be all hell to pay.'

'What?' cried Giles. 'Don't tell me your husband knows about all this!'

She turned and nodded. 'Of course. We don't have secrets from each other.'

'How many people know?' asked Giles.

'Simeon and I, the Gordons, you and Dominic.'

'And that's all?'

She paused, flashed a look at me, then looked up at Giles.

'Yes, that's all.'

'Right,' said Giles. 'Thank God. So once this furore over Wishart dies down and the news networks stop babbling about clones, Dominic will be safe to get on with his life. They haven't announced the sentence yet, and God knows I'm against executing people, but I hope they go for the maximum penalty with Wishart! The man's a monster.'

'Giles, they won't execute him!' cried Imogen.

'Professor Holt,' he said, 'you must know as well as I do that they probably will.'

And as we walked away and left her standing on the steps of her marble palace, I turned back to see her staring after us, her face full of fear.

22

Giles took me back to his house, a tall, old-fashioned terraced place with huge windows. I don't remember falling asleep but I'll never forget the waking on that first day of my new life.

My eyes opened onto a room full of dim, unfamiliar shapes. I struggled in my mind, stretching to reach the clues floating just outside my memory. Something had happened, something vast and unstoppable, but what?

I saw the outline of a man slumped in a chair near the bed. For long, fearful moments, I didn't know who he was, but as my eyes grew accustomed to the charcoal shades, I remembered Giles. And then I remembered why I knew him. My brother's best friend. And with a sudden sickening rush, all the new facts of my life came back.

I sat bolt upright and Giles woke.

'It's all right, mate, you're with me. It's Giles,' he said. 'You're quite safe.'

We looked at each other a while in the dimness.

At last, I managed to whisper, 'Is it true, what Imogen said?'

'Yes, it's true.'

'I feel so different,' I said. 'I don't know who I am any more.'

Giles went to draw back the curtains from two tall windows. Sunlight drenched the room. I felt the warmth of it.

'You are who you've always been.'

He came to sit on the bed and, for the first time, he

met my eye, smiled a different kind of smile. I suddenly thought that he would have smiled at Nick like this.

'I don't feel as if I am.'

A fly buzzed in the hot room.

'What time is it?' I asked.

'Umm . . . eleven.'

'Giles, did you know what I was?' I said. 'From the very first time you saw me?'

He looked up and the worry in his face made me panic. He was worried for me the freak, the unnatural being. Afraid for what would become of me.

'The first time you came to Grenville Hall?'

'Yes. Did you know already—about what Imogen had done?' I remembered his face peering up at me in the gloomy stairwell. He'd looked as if he'd seen a ghost.

'It was a shock seeing you,' he said, 'because you're so like him. To look at, I mean. But no—I didn't *know* about what Imogen had done, but . . . '

'But you guessed?'

He sighed. 'It wasn't such a hard guess to make. Gene therapy and the ethics of cloning were all part of what Nick was studying. And Imogen was—still is—one of the most brilliant geneticists in the world.'

He sprang off the bed as if he wanted to get rid of the whole idea. 'I thought, no, this is bizarre, it just isn't possible that Imogen would have done this to Nick. But of course I knew that it *was* theoretically possible. She could have done it. I just couldn't quite accept that she *would* have done it, knowing the penalty she would face if she was found out. I'd almost convinced myself that it was just an uncanny likeness, just coincidence. Lots of brothers look very alike. And then . . . when we saw the birthmark . . . '

'That proved it,' I whispered.

'Beyond doubt.'

'Becky knew it was proof too, didn't she?'

111

'Yes. It was a shock. Like me, she knew what was possible in theory, but she'd never in a million years have believed that Imogen would have actually gone ahead and done it.'

'And if it gets out, Imogen will face the death penalty.'

'Well, yes, in theory, but . . .'

'You said they'll execute Wishart.'

'I think they will, yes. It's the only way to enforce the global prohibition and deter others from attempting to clone an entire human. Wishart is the test case.'

'So they'd execute Imogen, if they found out?'

'It won't come to that.'

'It could, Giles, it could come to that! If they find out about me!'

I suddenly felt trapped in the bed. I threw back the covers and went to stare out of a window overlooking an ancient church. Gravestones were sticking up out of the long grass.

'You're right, it could,' said Giles. 'But as I said before, none of this is your fault!'

'That doesn't mean it isn't my problem! I just wish . . . I wish I'd never found out about it! It hasn't helped, me finding out the truth, it just makes it worse!'

'Makes what worse? What do you mean?'

'The whole thing with me and my father. When you said that just now about Imogen ''doing that to Nick'', it sounded as if it was a dreadful thing to do. It's all right, I know you didn't mean it to make me feel bad. But it *is* a dreadful thing to do. Imogen did it because she wanted to see if she could. That's bad enough. But my father did it because he wanted to replace Nick. Except it didn't work. I'm a duff copy. But he'll never stop trying to *make* me like Nick. He'll never accept that I just can't fit into the mould. There's nothing I can do to please him, ever. I don't want to see him again!'

Giles slumped back into the chair with a sigh.

'You don't have to see him yet if you don't want to,' he said. 'Tell you what . . . I mean, it's only an idea . . . how d'you fancy spending some time in Scotland, just while you get your head round all this? We were planning to go up there. A friend of ours has a cottage . . . '

'Who's "we"?' I asked. I didn't want to be amongst people.

'Well, Becky will come up at some stage,' he said, vaguely. 'She's gone away for a couple of days, so . . . '

'Will she want to, if I'm there?'

'Yes. It'll be fine,' he said.

I stared out at the gravestones again, the blazing sun on the lichen-stained church. I turned the idea over in my mind. I didn't know where I wanted to go and I remembered what Mum had written on that postcard to Giles: 'I don't really want to be anywhere'.

'Yeah,' I said, 'Scotland's as good as anywhere.'

'Right,' said Giles, standing up. 'There's no point in hanging around. We'll get going as soon as possible. I'll have to pop out and tie up a few loose ends. You . . . er . . . want some coffee? Breakfast?'

'Just coffee. I'm not hungry.'

He gave me a spare dressing gown and we went down to the kitchen. I sat at the table by an open window overlooking the walled garden. The breeze brought in a smell of herbs that hit me instantly with thoughts of Mum. She used loads of herbs in cooking and they were the only plants that she ever remembered to water and keep alive. I sniffed and saw her whirling around our kitchen, chopping ingredients, hurling them into pans to sizzle or steam, slurping her wine, waving her hands as she explained how flavours work together, her excitement when something came out just right.

'OK?' Giles plonked a mug down in front of me.

'I was thinking about Mum.'

'Give her a ring. Feel free to use the phone, won't you.'

'Thanks, but I've got my mobile.'

She could have phoned me. I'd check for messages when Giles was gone.

'No, use ours, it's cheaper,' he said. 'But probably best not to answer it if it rings. And don't answer the door. Make yourself at home of course, but . . . '

I shook my head. 'I won't.'

'OK. Anything else you need?'

'No—thanks.'

'I'll be back as soon as I can.'

And then he was gone in a flurry of briefcase and shopping bags and I was left alone in the silent house. I went back upstairs and checked my mobile. No new messages, not even from my father. Not from her.

I was angry. I wanted to hear what she had to say, for her to explain herself. I didn't want to believe that she had agreed to what my father and Imogen had done. But perhaps she had. I dialled the number and waited, feeling the harsh electronic purr vibrate from one silent house to another. She wasn't there. Stupidly, hoping I'd got the wrong number, I kept on and on trying, getting more and more angry with her for not being there and for being too forgetful to cope with a mobile like everyone else.

In the end, for want of anything better to do, I went to take a shower.

The white-tiled bathroom had a full-length mirror on one wall and shelves packed with creams and lotions, body scrubs, foam baths, and aromatic oils. Giles's shaving stuff was balanced on the side of the washbasin. As I closed the door I breathed in a peachy smell that I recognized as the perfume Becky had been wearing.

I turned on the shower and watched the needles of water hit the white porcelain in a building cloud of steam. I

114

looked at the mirror and saw myself wrapped in Giles's dressing gown, familiar skinny legs holding me up, familiar pale face and pale hair. I stared and stared at my face until I was frightened because I didn't know what I was looking at any more. It was the face of a stranger. I undid the dressing gown and let it fall to show the body I used to take for granted. Skinny limbs beginning to build muscle, chest broadening, everything happening as nature intended, so I used to suppose.

Behind me, the mirror above the basin showed me the mark on my back. A stab mark, it looked like. As the clouds of steam built and swirled, the person I was looking at ghosted in the mirrors.

This body that I used to know had lived as someone else before me and suddenly the horror ripped through me in a roar of rage and fear. I slumped onto the side of the bath, choking as the steam filled the room and filled my lungs, my chest heaving out of control, my nails gouging at the flesh on my legs as if I could tear it all off. I sat howling in desolate, bottomless rage.

A sudden draught of cooler air billowed the steam.

'Giles?' A panicky female voice came at me from the direction of the door.

I fell silent. She moved towards me. I saw the ghost of a red dress on a slim, dark-haired figure, dark eyes widening in horror as we recognized each other.

'Becky!'

I grabbed, too late, for Giles's dressing gown and held it over me, shivering despite the heat.

'What are you . . . what are you *doing* here?' she shrieked.

'I'm sorry . . . '

But, in a whirl of bright colour and steam, she was gone.

115

23

I reached the kitchen just as she bashed open the door
that led from there out to the garden. I watched her
stride down the brick path and stop suddenly, her
arms clasped low around her stomach as she bent into a
gentle rocking movement.

I knew she was crying for Nick. But I didn't know what
to do with all this misery, hers or mine. I didn't know
how to put it right. I watched her for a moment more and
then pushed at the door into the garden. I was no more than
a couple of paces down the path before she turned on me.

'Get back!' she spat. 'Get back into the house!'

'What?'

She flew at me and pushed me. We stumbled together
back into the kitchen and stood looking at each other. Her
almost-black hair broke loose from where she had tucked it
behind her ears, swinging forward along her jawline. She
tucked it back again furiously. Below the perfect line of her
collar-bone I half-saw the rise and fall of the breasts
beneath the thin red cotton. Her eyes flickered around my
face, settling for the tiniest moment in time, like a butterfly,
on my mouth.

'What are you doing here?' she said in a measured,
trembling voice. 'Why didn't Giles send you home?'

'He was just . . . I had nowhere else to go. I've seen
Imogen . . . Professor Holt. I know what happened, I know
about how she made me. You were right, what you saw,
the birthmark . . . ' I knew I wasn't making much sense.
There was something in her eyes that scrambled my

thoughts and words. 'I'll get my things. I didn't mean to hurt you. I didn't know the truth and I came looking for it and now I wish I hadn't!'

I was a couple of steps up the stairs when she stopped me.

'No,' she said, her nails digging into my arm. 'You're not going anywhere. I need to talk to you.'

She led me down the tiled passageway into the lounge, which was cool, untouched by the sun. She gestured to the sofa and sat beside me, twisting round to face me. I could see her heart beating overtime.

'I'm sorry,' she said. 'If this is difficult for me it must be a thousand times worse for you. What you must have felt when Imogen told you . . . '

'She didn't have to tell me. I'd already guessed,' I said. 'When people go to so much trouble to hide things and keep bursting into tears and running away and having rows about you, it sets you thinking. So I got it out of Imogen. Somatic cell nuclear transfer. I'm an expert now.'

She gave a weak smile and I guessed that this was the kind of smart-arse comment Nick would have made.

'It's really hard for me to get my head round the fact that Imogen really did it, that you're really here,' she said.

'Who do you mean when you say ''*you're* here''?' I asked.

Her eyes bored right into me in a way that sent a hot wave over my face and made me look away.

'Smart question. That's why I ran away, that's why I was frightened. I saw Nick. I didn't see *you*.'

'And do you now?'

She fixed me with a gentle shadow of a smile before looking away with a sigh.

'He's gone for ever, Dominic. This is *your* life, your opportunity to make choices. Nobody else's opportunity, nobody else's choices. But now that you know about what

Imogen did, you should know the rest. This is about much more than you and Nick and me and Giles. Did Giles tell you that I trained as a journalist?'

'No.'

'Well, I did. I don't do much in the way of pure journalism nowadays. Mainly I work on research with Giles. When he and I had our little row last night, I went to stay with a friend . . . '

'Why did you have a row?'

'At the time I thought it was because you phoned in the middle of the night and he ran off to get involved in something that was nothing to do with him. What I think *now* is that we argued because he's the best friend a person could have and I'm a selfish cow who can't sort her feelings out and behave like a grown-up. Will you shut up and listen?'

'Sorry.'

'My friend had some house-guests, a couple of journalists here for a big medical conference that starts on Monday— tomorrow. And at breakfast this morning everyone was talking about cloning—there's a doctor called Wishart who's been on trial in the European Courts . . . '

'I know,' I said. 'Giles told me.'

'OK. So, the point is that these journalists are asking themselves the question: if Wishart is capable of cloning a human—and we know he got as far as a viable embryo—who else is, and where did he learn the technique? And who has always led the field in a very closely related subject—therapeutic cloning and gene therapy?'

'Imogen.'

'Yes, Imogen. At the very least her views on the Wishart case will be sought. All the top medical journalists will be in Cambridge and they'll want to speak to her. That's OK as long as no one has reason to push things further, go digging

118

around for evidence that Imogen has actually cloned someone.'

'Would anyone have a reason?'

Becky sighed. 'I'm probably being too paranoid about the whole thing,' she said, 'but if anyone who knew Nick and knew how close he was to Imogen were to clap eyes on you at this moment—well, I'm just worried that it could happen. You look so like him, even though you're . . . how old are you?'

'Fifteen.'

'Just four years younger than Nick was when we first met.' Her smile brushed over me again. 'Anyway, think how much the story would be worth. A boy who's the spitting image of a student who just happened to die and who just happened to be Professor Holt's star pupil, from a very wealthy family—killed not long after the first successful adult cloning . . . '

'Then I'm not the first, there's someone else?' I cried.

'Not exactly. The first mammal to be cloned as you were was a sheep.'

'A sheep? I owe my existence to a sheep? Great!'

'That's one way of looking at it. I'm serious though, Dominic. It's not safe for you to hang around anywhere that Nick was known. The first journalist to find a living cloned person—and prove it—would make more money than you can imagine; but more importantly it would be the biggest scoop of the twenty-first century. The media would go crazy. You'd never be your own person again.'

'You think I should go home?'

'I think you should leave Cambridge.'

'You could prove it, though. You know everything.'

She put her trembling hand over mine.

'And you think I'd do that?' she said.

The front door banged and we heard the rustling of carriers and Giles cursing as he dropped some shopping. He appeared in the lounge doorway, clutching a burst bag of tomatoes to his chest. He looked nervously at Becky and me.

'Hello. You're back,' he said.

'Evidently,' smiled Becky.

'Is everything all right, then?'

'I hope it's going to be,' she said. 'I really hope so.'

24

Later that day, we decided to leave for Scotland first thing in the morning. If all went according to plan, said Giles, he wouldn't need to be back in Cambridge until the autumn term because most of his students were abroad for the summer doing field research.

'I'll keep in touch with them via email,' he said. 'And the couple that are staying in Cambridge won't need much help. They probably know more about the biodiversity of the rainforests than I do.'

'And I can do all my work on the laptop,' said Becky. 'So I'm as free as a bird—at least for a few weeks. Have you been to Scotland before, Dom?'

'No, never.' I was beginning to feel excited about the idea of going somewhere I'd never been and really exploring for myself.

'What did you say I should do with this?' asked Giles, waving a green chilli at me as I chopped vegetables. I'd offered to make one of Mum's specialities for our last supper in Cambridge.

'Take out all the seeds and chop it really finely,' I said.

'OK. Seeds out. Chop.' He cut open the chilli, then stuck a finger in his mouth and pulled it out again fast. 'Ow! That stings!'

'DON'T lick your fingers!' laughed Becky.

'And wash your hands *before* you have a pee!' I cried. 'Or it really *will* sting!'

A dishcloth flew across the kitchen and wrapped itself in a soggy slap around my face.

'Knew we should've stuck to omelette!' jeered Giles as I lobbed the dishcloth back at him. 'You can't get injured by an omelette!'

I stirred the sauce, conscious of my alien fringe flicking dark brown instead of blonde above my eyebrows. Giles and Becky thought I'd better dye my hair, just in case my father was still around. Or anyone else who might notice me. They'd both agreed that it might fool my father from a distance. Becky had also gone out and bought me a whole load of different clothes. I was a new man now. They weren't bad, although not exactly what I would have chosen. I'd buy some myself as soon as I could earn some money of my own.

'Smells gorgeous,' said Becky at my elbow.

I stirred the sauce again and sniffed.

'Needs a slosh of red wine if you have it,' I said.

She went off to find some and I stared into the pan, suddenly filled with misery as I thought again of Mum and all the cooking sessions we'd had together. I hadn't been able to get hold of her. All afternoon I'd tried, and again and again there'd been that ringing that felt so empty.

'This is one of your mum's recipes?' asked Becky, as if she had read my thoughts.

'Yeah.'

'Carla was always so kind to me,' she said, handing me the wine. 'Nick and I went to see her perform a couple of times.'

'What? When she was an opera singer?'

'Yes. She sings like an angel, your mum, doesn't she?'

Just what Pops was always saying. 'Sang. She doesn't any more,' I said.

'You still haven't been able to talk to her?' asked Becky, frowning.

'No. I've tried all day.'

'You know, I think you were right in what you said to

Imogen,' said Giles. 'I can't imagine your mother would have had much choice about what happened.'

'She should have stood up to him!' I cried, a lump hardening in my throat. 'If she really thought it was the wrong thing to do, she should never have agreed to have me! Anyway, it doesn't matter now. I'm going to start a new life—without either of them!'

I swallowed hard and hurled my chopped vegetables into the sauce.

'There,' I said, 'we can leave it to simmer now.'

I went to flop in the lounge and turned on the TV, desperate for some mindless pap to distract me. I flicked through the channels showing kids' stuff, cookery programmes, quiz shows—normal people doing normal things. Then came a news channel showing a crowd of demonstrators outside some swanky building. I was about to switch over when I saw the name on the placards that were being waved. The placards showed a balding man with a double chin, small, close-set eyes, and a broad smile. Underneath the picture was written 'Wishart must die'. Another one said 'Man can't play God!' The camera closed in on a reporter who was asking the opinion of an angry-looking woman.

'It's a wickedness!' she cried. 'It's against God's law to make children in this way. Thank the Lord the poor little thing was taken. It would have been a freak of nature! It wouldn't have grown up normal!'

'So you think Wishart should be executed?' asked the reporter.

There was a roar from the crowd behind her, people jigging placards up and down.

'Yes I do! The sooner the better!'

I stared at the woman. That was me she was talking about, 'a freak of nature', with her face all twisted up in anger.

Becky came in.

'Are you sure you want to watch this?' she said.

'Shhhhhh!' I nodded.

The camera cut back to the reporter and Becky came to sit beside me, leaning forwards, her face fixed on the screen.

'This is indeed a momentous time in the history of the European Court,' continued the reporter, 'and a test of its nerve. Parliament having set the death penalty as the ultimate sanction against the crime of cloning, can the Court now back down and show mercy to Wishart? Or will this be the first ever execution in twenty-first century Europe?'

As the reporter stepped away from the crowd to face the camera I had the feeling that I'd seen her somewhere before, although perhaps it was just the type of face and voice that all TV reporters seemed to have. She was explaining that Wishart's defence lawyers were arguing that because he hadn't actually succeeded in cloning a baby, the death penalty should not be imposed.

'The cloning procedure,' she explained excitedly, 'is simple in itself, but incredibly difficult to pull off. However, Wishart managed to get as far as a viable embryo, which then died in the womb. He *intended* to clone and, as far as the prosecution is concerned, that intention should earn him the lethal injection.'

A picture of a youngish couple flashed onto the screen. These were the people Wishart had been working for. They were super-rich. They'd got three boys already but they wanted a girl that looked exactly like the wife. She was a famous model, apparently, and she wanted her looks to live on.

The screen cut back to the demonstrators and now the reporter was talking to a priest. I shuddered. I had a pretty good idea what this wrinkly old man with his crucifix round his neck would say—more details of what God had to say on the matter, and it wouldn't be good. People behind him had started to scream. 'Execute *now*! Execute *now*!'

But the priest wasn't with the screaming people. The reporter managed to pull him away from the crowd so that we could hear what he was saying.

'I believe that cloning is inherently neither good nor evil,' he said in a shaky voice. 'Any person created through cloning would be a new person—a body, mind, and soul with experiences unique to themselves. Biologically, a clone is no different to an identical twin—albeit an identical twin born into another time and place. However, we should look not only at the biology but at the question of *intention*. What is intended when a child is created in this way? He or she is *intended* to be a copy of a person who has already lived. Therefore, I'm concerned about how such a child would be able to establish his or her own identity and whether those responsible for creating this child would recognize and respect that identity. My worry about cloning is to do with how such people would be treated. The cloned child would, after all, still be God's creature, deserving of compassion, of course he would, but if he were to be treated as a commodity or as a freak, a sub-human . . . '

'So you reckon it *wouldn't* be a freak?' yelled some red-faced guy behind him.

The crowd started up again, punching the air, shouting things about the death penalty, the Devil, God's Law. Goose pimples froze all over me as I watched the priest being stuffed into a car and driven away. Now the reporter was yelling, her voice triumphant, her face filling the screen.

'You heard it here first. A priest says that, had Wishart succeeded, the cloned child would still be God's creature. Well, we'll just wait and see what his superiors and the good people of his church have to say about that!'

The screen snapped into a commercial break. Three people in bear costumes singing some stupid song about a new kind of porridge.

I turned off the screen. All that screaming, all that anger at the *idea* of a clone. What would they do if they got hold of a real one? And there was another thing. I was pretty sure I remembered where I'd seen that reporter before.

'You two OK?' asked Giles from the doorway.

'Not really,' said Becky. 'There was a report from the European Court.'

'They're going to execute him?'

Becky shook her head. 'Not decided yet.'

'The fuss will die down once they have,' said Giles.

But I didn't think it would. Now that the thing was out in the open, everyone would have an opinion about cloning. The news stations, chat shows, and print news would churn out endless discussion. But nobody would know what it really meant. And as far as I knew, I was the only one that could tell them.

'Maybe,' said Becky. 'But guess who's in the thick of it, fronting the news report? Our dear friend Leanne Kelsey.'

Leanne Kelsey. So I was right, it *was* her, the woman I'd first seen in the library, the woman Giles and I had met yesterday on our way to the station. I looked up to see the shock on Giles's face.

'Oh God!' he said.

'What?' said Becky.

'She's seen Dominic. Yesterday. Only very briefly, but . . . '

'No! Oh, NO!' Becky flashed wide, frightened eyes from me back to Giles.

'But she might not have connected . . . ' he said.

'Giles, of course she will! She's paid to connect and she's damned good at it. Do you think she'd have forgotten what Nick looked like? She used to go out with him—she was besotted with him!'

'It's OK, Dom,' said Giles. 'We leave first thing in the morning. And we stay in Scotland until we're sure it's safe to come home, agreed?'

'Yeah,' I whispered, the terror pricking hot and cold all over me now. I caught Becky's expression and I knew she was thinking the same as me. The truth was, it might never be safe for me to go home.

25

I was just about to get into bed that night when the hammering began on the front door. Becky came running from the bathroom into my bedroom.

'Stay here,' she said. 'Whatever you do, don't come down until we know it's safe.'

She hit the light switch, leaving me in the dark as she ran down the stairs. I found the window and drew the curtain back a chink. A tall man was stepping through the front door below me. I flipped the curtain back into place and stood shaking in the darkness. I should have known my father would find me. I crept across to the door and strained to hear what was going on downstairs. There was the murmur of a voice, deeper than Giles's. Silently, I opened the door and took a few paces down the dark corridor.

'Does anyone else know about this?' The man's voice jabbed up from the hallway. Not my father. It was Simeon. 'You've kept the little bastard hidden, I hope.'

'Simeon, this situation is not of Dominic's making . . .' began Giles.

'Oh, I know whose *making* it is,' sneered Simeon. 'It's my wife's *making*. We'd better pray that no one's recognized him, because if anyone ever finds out . . .'

He looked up and saw me standing on the stairs. I saw his jaw muscles tense, the look of hot hatred.

'She wants to see you,' he said.

'You don't have to go,' said Becky.

'He does,' said Simeon. 'And after she's said whatever

it is she wants to say to him, he can get out of our lives for good.'

'Right,' said Giles. 'Then we're coming with him.'

'If you must,' said Simeon.

'Damned right we must!' cried Becky. 'And why this middle-of-the-night panic? What's happened?'

'Computer security has been breached at the Holt Foundation,' said Simeon. 'Someone's after Imogen.'

'What? I mean—how do you know it's that?' asked Becky.

'Well, what the hell else is it going to be?' He turned on her angrily.

'Calm down . . . ' said Giles.

'My wife's in line for a lethal injection and I'm supposed to *calm down*?' he shouted.

Giles moved to stand between him and me.

'Please. Just tell us what happened,' said Becky.

Simeon slid a look of disgust over me. Then he seemed to get a grip, turned back to Becky.

'They hacked into the system as far as security level two,' he said. 'That doesn't matter, as it happens, because all that research is in the public domain anyway. And they'd have found nothing about *him*, even on level one. Everything relating to his origins is on good old-fashioned paper.'

I remembered the safe in Imogen's underground lab, how she'd been locking something away in it just as I'd woken up.

'The point is that someone's digging around,' continued Simeon. 'Could be a government agency, the press, or someone Wishart has put on to her.'

'What do you mean, someone Wishart's put on to her?' snapped Becky.

'Wishart once worked for Imogen,' said Simeon. 'He was working with her when Dominic Gordon died.'

129

'WHAT?' yelled Giles. 'But she told us nobody knew . . . '

'He was working on an unrelated project,' said Simeon, 'but it's just possible that he might have known something. And if he did and he chooses to talk in the hope of saving his own neck . . . '

'Was he with her in the Cayman Islands?' I said.

'Very briefly,' he replied, without even looking at me.

'And would he have seen my parents there?'

This time he did look at me, that look of disgust again, as if I was worthless, a nothing.

'Imogen doesn't think there'd have been any reason for their paths to cross, but she can't remember,' he said.

'Did Wishart know Nick?' I asked Becky.

'Not to my knowledge. But Nick's death was high-profile news in Cambridge for a time. And of course your father's a prominent business figure and Carla was carving out her opera career. None of them was exactly inconspicuous—it's just a question of whether Wishart ran into them around that time and whether he would have reason to suspect what Imogen was up to.'

We all knew what she was thinking. She'd said it before. A brilliant young life snuffed out, a wealthy couple grieving for their only son . . . they go on holiday with Professor Holt and nine months later they have another son.

'Exactly,' said Simeon. 'If anyone stitched together the right facts and then happened to catch sight of *him* . . . '

'But they'd need proof that Nick and Dom are . . . that they both have the same DNA,' said Giles.

'Which is precisely what they're not going to get,' said Simeon.

'If Wishart is behind this,' said Becky, 'he won't let it go. Dragging Imogen into it is his only chance of escaping the death penalty. What court is going to order the execution

130

of the woman who made paraplegics walk again? And if they won't execute her, they can't execute him!'

'NOBODY is going to drag my wife into anything!' cried Simeon.

We stood in the dark hallway, silent seconds passing. Simeon's best way out would be to get rid of me permanently, any idiot could see that.

'When Imogen's finished her little chat, what then?' said Becky.

'I want him out of our lives,' said Simeon. 'And if I ever set eyes on him again . . . '

He didn't need to say it. There was no death penalty for murder.

'Right,' said Giles. 'We were leaving in the morning anyway. Just wait while we get our stuff together. Once he's seen her, you can drop us all at the nearest Link, can't you?'

'Yeah, whatever,' said Simeon. 'Just hurry it up!'

We got dressed and shoved the last of our packing into the bags. When I got back downstairs Simeon was waiting, alone. He turned away from me.

'I'm still a person, you know!' I said.

He didn't answer. Becky came running down the stairs with some bags and Giles arrived from locking up the back. We left the house and walked to where Simeon had left Imogen's chauffeur-driven car, a couple of streets away. There was no chauffeur this time, though. Simeon drove us himself and all the time, as we slid almost silently through the quiet back streets of Cambridge, he was watching, flicking nervous glances at the rear-view mirror. We drove out into the main part of town and I sank down in the back next to Becky, hardly daring to look through the tinted window as we passed bright lights, pumping music, and groups of laughing students clustered around pub doorways. I felt it all wash by, this happy world of normal people, until we left it behind and headed out into dark countryside.

26

O nce we were clear of the city, the car sped along and a feeling of panic tightened in my stomach.

'I want to speak to Imogen!' I cried.

'You're going to speak to her, you little prat,' said Simeon, hurling the car into a bend and slamming down a gear.

'No, I mean now! Stop the car! Give me her mobile number!'

'Oh, so you don't trust me,' laughed Simeon. He accelerated hard, the force pinning me back against the seat.

'Slow down!' said Giles. 'It won't help if you crash the car!'

'He's going to kill us anyway, Giles!' I cried.

'I might just do that if you don't shut up! Jesus! Thank God we've got no kids!'

Becky found my hand. I turned to her.

'It's OK,' she whispered. 'Imogen won't let him . . .'

We were thrown together as the car slid round a really sharp bend. Simeon regained control and we sped off again. It wasn't OK. Everything was wrong. I watched the feathery oak silhouettes zip by, then dark flat land. Nowhere to hide in such a landscape. You'd soon be hunted down. And more than anything at that moment I wanted to run, run, run . . .

Soon the car slowed, then swung suddenly into the gateway of a field. The headlamp beams bounced as the car joggled over the baked earth, heading for a dark shape in the mid-distance that looked like a huge barn. Simeon pulled up outside it. It was an aircraft hangar. One huge door was open and a fire glowed just inside.

'She's in there,' said Simeon.

'D'you want me to come with you?' said Becky.

'She wants to see him alone,' said Simeon.

'I'm more interested in what Dom wants,' said Becky, 'if you don't mind.'

'I'll go alone,' I said.

I slammed the car door behind me and scrunched across the stubble towards the light of the fire. I didn't even know why I was doing this. What did I want to hear? 'We were only joking, you're not really a clone, ho, ho, that really got you going . . . ' There wasn't anything she could say to take the nightmare away.

I stepped into the hangar. It seemed empty apart from her and her fire, although you couldn't really tell because the fire only lit up the area around the door. The air was hot and musty. She was feeding papers into the flames. She looked up.

'You wanted to see me?' I said.

'Come and sit,' she said.

I declined the offer.

'How are you?' she said.

'Oh, fine, just fine,' I said.

'I'm sorry you're angry.'

'Why wouldn't I be? It's not so great knowing your whole life is just someone else's experiment.'

'Please come and sit.'

She looked tired. She shrugged slightly and turned back to her pile of documents. The flames roared hungrily as she fed them more paper.

'That's the good thing about paper,' she said. 'No one can hack into it and it's wonderfully combustible.'

'That's the stuff about me and Nick, I suppose,' I said.

133

She nodded. 'Yes.'

We watched the flames. When she looked up, her face had changed. She wasn't the cool, genius professor any more. She looked almost frightened. She spoke softly and quickly.

'Dominic, sixteen years ago, when I did what I did, I didn't see what the real consequences might be. I let an arrogant, ruthless man get the better of my judgement. I allowed him to exploit my curiosity as a scientist. Could this thing be done with a human? I was sure it could, and I wanted to be the first to do it. At the time I didn't think about Carla, or, if I did, I just thought she ought to be grateful to get her son back. I didn't think about *who* that son would be . . .'

'Well, you're in good company there,' I said. 'Nobody else thought about who I'd be either. They just assumed I'd be Nick.'

She smiled. 'And you've proved us wrong.'

'And how do you work that one out? How can I prove anything, how can I be certain about anything? I don't know who I am any more! There is no "me"!'

'Of course there is. Think about it!' she said.

'What do you mean?'

'I mean, who do you think you are?' she grinned.

'It's not bloody funny!' I yelled. 'I've got his flesh and blood and bones and hair and eyes and even the damned birthmark!'

'That's pretty well true,' she said. 'That's what I cloned. But that's all.'

'That's *all*?' I cried. 'It's enough, isn't it?'

'No,' she said, 'it's nowhere near enough to make a human being, and you know it.'

We stared at each other. I was shaking with rage.

'What do I know?'

'You *know* who you are, Dominic. You cannot make a

copy of a human being. You can copy their DNA—that is, you can copy the body the person had as a baby . . . '

Her eyes were glittering and I suddenly remembered where I'd seen eyes of that colour before. They were the precise colour of a lioness's eyes.

'But you can't copy their mind,' I said. 'Is that what you mean?'

'That's it. That's exactly it! Everything your senses have absorbed, every emotion you've ever experienced, every connection you've ever made about how the world around you works . . . it's all gone into making YOU! I couldn't copy that. No one ever could. The human brain is the most complex mechanism on earth, Dominic, and we each have to live with our own.'

'You're talking about consciousness,' I said.

'Yes.'

She leaned towards the fire and began feeding in the papers again. 'The last of my papers on you and Nick,' she said. A strand of her hair swung forwards and I leaned over to pull it back for her, suddenly full of fear with the idea that she might go up in flames too.

We watched the flames as they screwed the papers into charred rags. Twisting, billowing, and sparking. So many shapes, so many rhythms, so many colours.

'No two ever the same,' I said.

'Exactly,' she said. She turned and dragged a bag towards her. I saw that it was my rucksack. 'You left your things behind,' she said. 'Don't you want to keep the paints?'

She smiled at me, the flames snapping red and gold lights on and off all over her face. And then her face changed and her eyes filled with tears. 'I'm sorry. I'm really sorry. But this is for the best!'

A tiny flick of her gaze to something behind me made me spin round. I heard what sounded like a metal door closing at the dark end of the hangar and the gritty scrape

135

of footsteps coming closer. My father stepped into our circle of light.

'Oh, no! NO! You bitch!' I cried.

'I had to Dominic! It's the only way you'll be safe!'

'We're going home now, Dominic,' said my father.

I spun round to the other door and saw Simeon guarding it. But there was still a chance I could get through. My father switched on a torch and its powerful beam showed the door through which he'd come.

'This way,' he said, picking up my rucksack and slinging it over his shoulder. 'The helicopter's waiting on the other side. Thank you, Imogen, and goodbye.'

I ran towards Simeon, meaning to dodge round him at the last minute. Imogen screamed 'No!' and I saw Simeon raise his arm. I put on a spurt to get round him and then suddenly I was on the ground, a hot pain searing my left calf. The sound seemed to come just as I'd fallen, a muffled punch of sound. I clamped a hand to my calf and found it was wet. Imogen was screaming, louder and louder.

'Drop the gun, Simeon! Drop it! *Please!*'

I looked up at Simeon and saw him lower the hand that held the gun. 'Next time I won't miss!' he shouted. 'Now get him in the damned helicopter while you've still got the chance.'

An arm round my waist dragged me to stand on my remaining leg and my father's voice, hot against my ear, said, 'Come on, you little idiot!'

I tried to kick and elbow him off me but the pain was pumping in the leg that had been shot. It was hard to breathe. I felt myself being dragged into the darkness, away from the dying glow of the fire, as my vision began to fade. From somewhere near the fire came a strange sound, almost like an animal howling.

A long time afterwards I realized what that sound must have been. It was Imogen crying.

27

I dreamed I was lying on a couch in a laboratory and there were people crowded all round me. Hands were coming out to touch me in a way that felt like a shoal of fish nibbling at my skin but I couldn't move myself to sit up and see what they were doing. Some of the people were doctors with masks and then suddenly I understood that they were taking tiny scrapes from my skin, tiny slivers which they put onto slides and held up to the light. Sample after sample, so that soon my skin would be all stripped off. They started to argue about what the slides meant. They started to ask me questions, wiring me up with microphones so that everything I said could be heard. A sudden excitement broke through the crowd and the doctors turned into TV interviewers and reporters and then some of them grabbed at the side of the couch, which turned into a trolley and I was being pushed, faster and faster towards blinding halogen lights. I arrived in some sort of studio with flashlights going off all around me. I was pulled into a sitting position and a woman was rubbing make-up into my face, getting me ready for the giant cameras that I could just see beyond the lights, while all around babbling voices, barking to be heard over each other, were hurling questions, questions, questions . . .

The make-up began to burn into my skin and every time the blinding lights flashed the pain burned deeper. I was screaming at them all to turn off the lights.

I woke, sweating, with the terror of the dream dragging through me like an outgoing wave, my heartbeat pounding hard. I was in a bright room. Gradually I took in the fact that there were medical instruments all round me. Things with tubes and dials.

'No!' I cried out in terror. The nightmare was real. The instruments were real. I was in a hospital bed.

Someone moved to my side and a firm hand grasped my arm.

'Stay still. Completely still.'

She was a plump woman in a white coat.

'You're not experimenting on me! You are NOT going to touch me!' I yelled.

'Shush, now, Dominic. No one's going to harm you.'

I tried to sit up and she leant over me to hold me down. I could feel her chest pressing down on me, could smell her clinical breath.

'It's very important that you listen to me, Dominic,' she said. 'You're at home. There's nothing to worry about. But you mustn't move. We weren't expecting you to come round quite so soon. I'll call your mother and she can explain.'

She released me and got a mobile from her pocket.

'Young Dominic is awake,' she told the phone. 'Would you like to come down?'

I turned my head and saw that I was in fact at home, as the nurse had said. The bed was in the middle of the summer lounge and most of the other furniture had gone. Sunlight glared through the huge patio doors.

'What are all these things doing here?' I asked the nurse.

'Just a few things to help us keep an eye on you,' she said. 'This machine monitors your blood pressure. There's one drip for the pain-killer and one for nutrition. Over here is a mobile scanner so that we can keep your father updated on your healing process.'

I remembered the shooting and tried to move my left leg.

'What's happened to my leg?' I cried. I couldn't move it. I couldn't even feel it.

The door opened and there was Mum.

'Mum! My leg! I can't feel it!'

I tried to haul myself up on my elbows but the nurse pushed me down again.

'Keep still, darling!' cried Mum.

'He's cut my leg off!' I began crying.

'Your leg is fine,' said Mum. 'At least, it will be if you do as you're told.'

She came to stand by the bed. She looked awful—her face was pale and thin and the energy that I knew as Mum had all drained away. She had torn herself to pieces, I could tell.

'It's important that you keep still,' she said. She was wearing some sort of pale, shapeless dress instead of her usual bright colours. She took my hand. I could feel her shaking.

'If you'd like to go and get a coffee,' she said to the nurse.

'I might as well take my lunch break—if you don't mind,' she said.

'Fine,' smiled Mum.

We waited for her to go, then Mum turned to me.

'Why can't I feel my leg?' I cried.

'It's in a brace,' she said. 'You should be able to feel it, though.' Her eyes were wide and anxious. 'Are you sure you can't?' She turned back the bottom of the bedclothes and I felt her cool hand on the toes of my left foot.

'Yes, I can feel that!' I relaxed back onto the pillow.

'There were complications with the gunshot wound,' said Mum. 'Your father and the doctors were worried about blood clots. It's crucial that you keep absolutely still until the clots have broken down naturally.'

'How long have I been here?'

'Ten days,' she said.

'And what happens if I don't keep still?' I said.

Her eyes filled with tears. 'Oh, Dominic, please, please do as we ask!'

Blood clots. I remembered. It was a blood clot that had killed my brother.

'Mum.' I found her hand. 'Don't . . .'

'Imogen called me,' she said. 'She told me that you'd found out.'

'And you told Dad, and he kidnapped me and nearly got me killed,' I said.

I was beginning to feel my leg now. It was heavy and stiff, and somehow it felt as if it wasn't mine any more.

'Darling, we both love you,' said Mum. 'We're trying to do what's best for you.'

'Then try something else, because this isn't working! You can't go on pretending I'm Nick—or wishing I was.'

She squeezed my hand. 'Dominic, I'm sorry. Of course you're angry and I don't know what to do to help you understand, to explain. There *is* no explanation, except . . . There's something that happens to you when you have a child. Suddenly you're not just you any more, not just a single life. Suddenly there's someone else's life that's far, far more important than your own. This precious life is at the very centre of your being, and you know that you would die for him and if necessary you would kill for him. The love is immeasurable, Dominic. And if you lose that child, the grief is indescribable. You would do *anything* . . .'

'But you could never replace him, Mum!'

'I know that,' she said, tears trickling down her colourless cheeks.

'You could have had another baby, a different baby,' I said. But I saw the answer in her face. I knew it, anyway. 'It was Dad, wasn't it? Dad didn't want another baby. He wanted his trophy son back!'

140

'He refused to accept that Nick was dead,' she said, her voice quiet and shaken. 'He never really took it in. He didn't break down, he didn't grieve in the way I did. Instead, he shut himself off completely—it was as if he was in another place, another time. And you *are* in a sort of no-man's land when somebody so close dies. The real world around you doesn't seem to have any meaning or purpose any more. It seems incomprehensible that it can all go on as normal—people going to work, shopping, laughing, and having fun—when your world has stopped dead. Except his no-man's land was different, I think, because he just couldn't accept that this pain was his to bear, and that there was no avoiding it. At times, he'd behave as if nothing had happened at all. And then suddenly, within days of Nick's death, he'd made up his mind what he was going to do about it. He thought it could be fixed, you see. He began talking to Imogen, trying to persuade her to . . . '

'Go on, say it, Mum—to make a replacement!' I said.

'He knew that Imogen's work with paraplegics involved stem cell research and that this meant cloning embryos up to a certain stage of development. He knew that if such a cloned embryo were to develop to full term, then . . . yes, in theory, a dead person . . . ' her voice wavered, 'a dead person could be brought back to life. That's what he believed. It was his way of dealing with the grief.'

'And did you believe that too?'

'I didn't know . . . I didn't think. All I knew was that I wanted to hold my son in my arms again. But as you grew I could see that I had a new son, a different son. Your father couldn't see this. He didn't want to see it. I know that I should have left him, I should have taken you away, but I was afraid he'd find us. I was too afraid to do what was right for *you* and . . . and I'm not very good at living with the guilt of that failure. That's the truth.'

141

I stared at the ceiling, terrified. I'd always known that my mother fell to pieces and hit the booze on a regular basis, but she'd always managed to pull things together somehow and we'd coped with my father together. But now, because of all this, things had changed. It meant we couldn't go on pretending that there was nothing wrong— and pretending was the one thing that had kept us going.

'Everything's changed,' I said feebly.

'Darling, it's not that your father doesn't love you,' said Mum.

'Oh, please! Don't defend him, Mum!' I said. 'If you love someone then you accept who they are! He's not interested in finding out who I am. Where is he, anyway, the invisible puppeteer? Thanks to him I could have been killed, not that he'd care!'

'Oh, Dominic, don't! He'd never let anyone hurt you.'

'He wasn't the one with the gun.'

She didn't answer, just kept stroking my hand, the tears still rolling.

'Mum, we could still do it. We could get away from him,' I said.

She shook her head. 'It's too late, Dominic—too late for that now.'

'What d'you mean?' I cried. 'Mum?'

A sudden draining feeling rushed through me, sucking all my energy away.

'Mum! What's happening!' I grabbed at her hand. 'I feel . . .'

'It's all right. It's the sedative. It's coming through the drip in your arm. To keep you still. We shouldn't have to do this for much longer. I promise you, everything will be all right soon . . .'

Her voice floated away from me.

I don't know how many days it was that I drifted in and out of consciousness. I remember hearing my father say that I was too headstrong for my own good and the nurse replying that it was easy enough to keep me quiet until the time came. I remember Mum holding my hand.

I awoke, finally, with a feeling that things were about to change. The drip that had been in my arm was gone and my head felt clearer. My leg had been released and I could wiggle my toes. There were some crutches leaning against the end of the bed.

'Your father will see you tomorrow,' said the nurse. 'When he's back from making all the arrangements.'

'What arrangements?' I said.

'Expect he'll want to tell you all about it himself.' She smiled.

Mum came into the room.

'Is it true he wants to see me?' I asked. 'I don't want to see him!'

I struggled to a sitting position and, through the patio doors, I saw my father's helicopter sitting at the end of the long sweep of lawn.

'Darling, please, you've got to listen to what he's going to say,' said Mum. She threw a glance at the nurse, who collected a bag and left the room.

'Why's the helicopter here?' I asked.

'It's been here ever since he brought you home,' said Mum.

'But *he's* not here?'

'No. He's coming back tomorrow,' she said.

'And what if I don't want to listen to what he's got to say?' I said. 'Don't tell me—the ultimate punishment. If I don't play ball he'll have me wiped out and re-cloned.'

'Are you going to try your crutches?' she said.

'No. What's the point? I might as well be paralysed anyway! What's this about "arrangements" he's supposed to be making?'

'We're going to Australia,' she said. 'All of us.'

143

'What? How long for?'

'For good. He wants to make a new start.'

I stared in disbelief at her drawn face.

'Australia? Why?' I cried.

'Dominic, do you have any idea of what will happen if the media finds out about you? They'll tear you to shreds.'

'I know, I've seen it,' I said. '"Unnatural, a freak", that's what people would say I am.'

'Please, please go along with what your father says!' she grabbed me, squeezed my arm hard. 'Just do it. We can all go to Australia and you can pretend to toe the line. Then, when you're grown-up you can do what you like. But for now, he's the only person who can protect you. Please, Dominic, do it for me! I'm so frightened! Why do you think he's left the helicopter here? There's a pilot on standby too. He knew we might have to get out of here at a moment's notice—to get you to the airport if the press found out about you. I don't want to live in fear like that!'

I felt again those hands from the dream. Nibbling fish, eating me away in little bites.

'You know that I love you more than anything, don't you?' she said.

'I know,' I said, flopping back onto the pillow.

So I'd do what she wanted. I didn't have a choice anyway. If my father was so afraid of what might happen that he was prepared to move to Australia, things must be really bad.

She brushed her hand against my cheek and gave me that look that I knew so well. I'd never really understood the mix of this expression before, but now I did. It was love, sorrow, and fear.

28

Later that morning, after I'd had a breakfast of yoghurt, bread, and honey, I sat up and pulled the bedclothes off me. My legs looked pale and wasted against the white sheet, as if they had been leached of life. I moved my right knee up and then my left. I leant down to examine the dressing, pressing on it gingerly. I couldn't feel any pain.

'No, Dominic, your father says not to touch the dressing,' said the nurse, turning from some papers at the other end of the room.

'Why?' I said.

'Best not to disturb it,' she said.

'I want to get up,' I said.

'Very well.' She came towards me but by the time she reached me I had swung my legs over the edge of the bed and my feet had found the floor.

'Take things very slowly,' she said. 'Remember you've been lying down for a fortnight and you've been fed through a drip. It'll take time to recover your strength.'

'Are there any clothes for me?'

'Here's a dressing gown,' she said.

I caught her glance as I put the dressing gown on, and got the feeling that she didn't want me moving about but she knew she couldn't stop me.

'Careful!' she snapped as I eased myself onto my feet.

My legs felt very weak. I stood for a few seconds and then sat back on the bed again.

'Can I have the crutches, please?' I said.

145

She handed them over and I slipped my arms into the armrests, took a firm hold and tried again. I discovered that if I took most of my weight on the crutches it was not too bad. My right leg could take a little weight and I decided to work on that. No way was I going to be a sitting duck when my father got back tomorrow.

I did a couple of slow circuits of the room, stopping every so often to test the left leg.

'Can I go out?' I asked the nurse.

'Well—the fresh air would do you good, I suppose. But you must take it very gently. Just a few steps and you can rest on the bench outside in the sun. That'd be nice, wouldn't it?'

She opened the patio doors and I made my way out onto the lawn. Way down at the end of our grounds was the helicopter, like a huge sleeping insect, its blades slightly drooped. I stood blinking in the sunlight and tried to take in what it would mean, going to a new country and starting again, this time with a secret that could never be told. I wanted to call Indy, Steve, Pogo, or even Zita . . . but what could I say? I didn't want to have to make up a whole story about why we were going. I didn't want to talk to anyone if I couldn't tell the truth.

I swung off across the lawn, moving quite fast once I'd got a rhythm going, using my good leg and the crutches.

'Dominic!' I heard Mum's panicky voice calling from her bedroom window. 'Stay there!'

A moment later she came running towards me.

'Why the hell aren't you watching him?' she yelled at the nurse.

The nurse looked annoyed. 'He was told to take it gently! I can't be responsible if he disobeys!'

Suddenly the ground beneath me tipped violently and I fell. I lay on the hot grass as the lawn swirled around with me on it. Mum threw herself down beside me.

'Faint!' I managed to whisper.

'Of course you'll feel faint if you go tearing off like that!' she said. 'Oh, Dominic, what are we going to do with you? Lie still. Deep breaths now.'

I lay there, fighting my body, willing myself not to pass out. I concentrated on the bright, crinkly leaves of the tree above me. It was an oak. One day, I thought, Nick's oak tree, the one that Giles planted for him, will be as big as this one.

'What time's he coming back?' I whispered.

'Tomorrow evening. We'll be flying out the following morning,' said Mum.

'I'm not going to be some bloody invalid at his mercy,' I said.

'You won't be.' She stroked my hair. 'We'll cope, Dominic, you and I. We always have. There's an exciting new life ahead.'

I took a deep breath of the warm, grass-scented air.

'If you say so,' I murmured.

A shadow moved over me and I heard the nurse's voice.

'Come along now, Dominic!'

The next thing I knew, I was back in bed.

29

That evening after supper, I tried again. I wasn't going to wreck my chances this time. I did as I was told and walked up and down a few times outside the lounge, then rested on the bench.

Next morning, the morning of the day my father was due back, I ate what was given me for breakfast and asked for more bread and jam, reckoning that carbohydrate and sugar would do me good. I was beginning to feel stronger. After breakfast I walked again, this time quite a bit further.

Around mid-morning, I set off to do a circuit round the outside of the house. Next to the summer lounge was the dining room and as I glanced in through the window I saw that the room had been stripped bare. A few packing crates stood in the centre, where the table had been. That was all. I moved on to the main lounge. The patio doors were open and I went in to find Mum standing at the shelves where she kept her music collection. Just one shelf of CDs remained. Almost everything had been cleared out of here too—only the sofa bed and a few crates were marooned in the centre of the vast room.

'Hello, darling!' She spun round with a smile. She'd got a new dress and her face was made up almost like her usual self.

'You look nice,' I said.

'I'm feeling better,' she said. 'If you get better, I'll get better. How's the walking going?'

'Not bad,' I said.

As I came to stand beside her I caught a faint whiff of alcohol. So that was why she was feeling better.

'I was just . . . ' she quickly closed the CD case she had been holding and slotted it into a box alongside dozens of others, but not before I'd seen the title.

'*The Marriage of Figaro*. Isn't that one of your favourites?' I picked up the CD.

'Oh, I have many favourites. Put it back now, Dom, I've got a lot of packing to get through.'

I opened the case and looked at the pictures and the blurb.

'Mum, this is you!' I cried in amazement. 'I've never seen this before!' I sat down on the sofa bed and looked at the cast list. Susanna was played by Carla Richardson. Opposite was a picture of Mum, all done up in a brightly-coloured dress, her hair curled, her heavily made-up eyes huge and full of life.

'Mum, I never knew about this! Can we play it?' I said.

'NO!' she snapped. 'Maybe one day, but not yet. I can't . . . I just don't want to hear it.'

Just as she said this, my hungry eyes found the recording date. It had been recorded in 2000.

She came to sit beside me.

'Nick and Becky came to see me in the opening night of that production,' she said. 'The summer of 2000. Such a happy time . . . '

'Then why can't you play it?'

'It's a strange coincidence, you picking out this one, now that we're going to Australia,' she went on, as if she hadn't heard me. 'Because I would have gone to Australia then. After we opened in London we were supposed to run right through to Easter . . . Easter 2001 . . . and then we were due to go on tour, starting in Australia, at the Sydney Opera House.'

'But then Nick died—in February,' I said.

'Yes. And I didn't want to sing. To me, music is about expressing what it's like to be alive, and all my life was gone—there wasn't any music left in me. My understudy took over and did the tour.'

She got up and went back to her shelves.

I stared miserably at the picture of Mum in her bright dress. It wasn't true that she loved me more than anything. Nothing could ever come close to what she felt about Nick.

'Will you ever sing again?' I asked.

'I don't know,' she said. 'It's probably too late now.'

I closed the CD case and put it back in the box.

'I'm going to make a phone call,' I said.

'What? Oh—you can't,' she said.

'Why not?'

'The phone has been disconnected—you know—because we're leaving.'

'Then I'll use my mobile. Where's my rucksack?'

'Oh dear—I think it's been packed.' Her eyes shifted from me. She was bad at lying and we both knew it.

'Mum, stop it! Tell me the truth!'

She buried her face in her hands for a second, then came up to look at me.

'Your father doesn't want you phoning anyone. It's got to be that way until we're safely in Australia. In a couple of weeks, once we're settled, you can call Steve and Pogo and whoever else you want to and explain that . . . oh, God, I don't know, Dom. Your father will know what's best to say. It's not that unusual. People uproot all the time to go to other countries—for loads of reasons.'

I slumped back onto the sofa bed with that familiar feeling of being out-witted, that he was trying to second-guess things about my life. Maybe he'd reckoned on there being no one who'd really miss me. And maybe he was wrong.

150

'Mum, you *must* let me phone Giles! He and Becky cared about me, they wanted to help me. Last thing they knew, Simeon shot me and I disappeared in a helicopter. Suppose they called the police?'

'They wouldn't, though, would they?' she said.

We looked at each other. It was true. The very last thing Giles and Becky could have done was to go to the police.

'But that's all the more reason I should ring them,' I said. 'They'll be worried and there's nothing they can do to find out if I'm OK.'

She still looked uncertain.

'All right then,' I said. 'Just get my mobile and *you* can ring them!'

She nodded. 'Giles was such a good friend. You're right. He deserves to know you're safe. I'll get the mobile.'

'Just bring my rucksack,' I said.

I went out onto the lawn and started my walking practice again. The left leg was getting stronger—nowhere near full strength, but at least I could stand on it for a few seconds without the crutches.

Mum came back with my rucksack and I sat down on the bench and fished out the mobile and the card Giles had given me.

'Do you want to ring him?' I held out the phone for her.

She shook her head. 'No, don't be silly—you speak to him.'

I dialled Giles's mobile number. *Please* be there, Giles, *please*. The phone's purring sounded very faint. I wondered where he was. Were they in Scotland now?

'Hello.'

It was Becky's voice.

'Becky?' Relief washed over me. It was as though her voice was proof that an outside world existed. 'It's me, Dominic.'

'Dominic! We've been so worried! We didn't know how to reach you! Are you all right?'

'I'm fine. My leg's fine. I'm at home. And you?'

'We're in Scotland. Can you talk?'

'No, not at all,' I said breezily. 'I'm just calling to say that we're going to Australia . . . ' I caught Mum's eye, ' . . . for a while. We're just going over for a while.'

'And not coming back?' said Becky.

'No,' I said.

'Dominic, that may be a good thing,' she said. 'You'll be safer there. Everything's going crazy here. Have you seen the news?'

'No.'

'Wishart has been sentenced to death. There's a whole load of speculation in the media about whether any other scientists might have tried to clone a human. I haven't come across any suggestion that Imogen might have been involved, but after that break-in at the Holt Foundation, we can't be sure that no one's on to her.'

'So you think Australia is the right thing?' Hearing the worry in her voice made my own voice shaky.

'I do. For the moment.' She sounded sad and washed-out. 'But, Dominic, you will keep in touch, won't you?'

'I will,' I said. 'Goodbye, Becky.'

I pressed the red key, cutting off Becky's forlorn voice as she said goodbye. I looked up at Mum.

'She thinks it's a great idea—to go to Australia,' I said.

'It is, I'm sure of it,' she said.

30

We had lunch in the kitchen. Mum did one of her pasta things with home-made sauce. She was chattering away, some of her liveliness returning, probably because of the booze she was knocking back. Or perhaps because she was so relieved that I was going to play ball. Every last detail had been planned. My father would be home tonight and tomorrow morning early we'd drive to the airport. Everything that I would need had been packed for me. My new school was the best in Sydney and it was expected that I would make it to one of the top universities.

'After that,' beamed Mum, 'you'll be a free man.'

I tried to feel happy for her. For us. Maybe they were all right—it would be the best thing, this new start. And there were landscapes and animals and plants that I'd always wanted to see for myself.

'They say there's a great social life in Sydney too,' she said. 'We'll both find loads of new friends!' She gave another little grin and I felt awful about bursting the bubble, but I had to ask.

'Mum, what about Pops?'

Her face fell. She put down her fork and reached out for her glass.

'Margi will make sure he's all right,' she said.

'Mum, he's eighty-two years old! He needs his family!'

'He'll have a family . . .'

'What do you mean?'

'Dom, we can't take him with us! He'd be confused . . .'

153

'What do you mean, he'll have a family?'

Suddenly the door behind me opened with a soft brushing noise over the thick carpet. I saw Mum glance up fearfully and I turned my head to see my father. I shouldn't have been surprised. I pushed my plate away as he joined us at the table, bending to kiss Mum on the head before he sat.

'Hello, Dominic,' he said.

'Hello.' Suddenly I felt queasy again, either because of the food or because of him. The smell of his aftershave swept across the table.

'How's the leg? Healing nicely?'

'Yes. Lucky he didn't aim for the chest. Or perhaps he did. Perhaps he's just a lousy shot.'

'Dominic, we owe you an apology for all that's happened,' he said. 'And the first thing I want to say is that if you'd like your grandfather to join us in Australia, then of course that can be arranged, if he's fit enough to travel and he wants to come.'

This was the last thing I'd expected and I couldn't think of anything to say. I just nodded and said, 'OK.'

He gave me one of those crisp little smiles that always meant that the subject was finished with.

'I must say I'm rather looking forward to retiring,' he said brightly. 'Needless to say we shall all be starting life afresh under new identities. The opportunities for you will be marvellous, Dominic, and I hope they will go some way towards making up for the upset you've had. Perhaps we should have told you about Nick. However, that's all in the past. You must look to your new life. It has taken a fair amount of organization and has cost a lot of money; however, everything is in place now.'

I looked at Mum's anxious smile. It struck me that I must have been a pretty expensive project all round. My father continued, 'I also want to say, Dominic, that I'm sorry about the manner in which I was obliged to remove you from Cambridge.'

'You're *sorry*?' I cried. 'Oh, don't mention it! I just love being shot at! Did you *know* he had a gun?'

'Of course not!' he snapped. 'For God's sake, do you think I'd have risked your life? But I hope it's been a lesson about what happens when you meddle in things you don't understand. We had to do something. We couldn't afford to have you blundering about in Cambridge much longer. The timing of your discovery couldn't have been worse. Things could become very, very dangerous, for reasons which I'll explain once we're safely away from here.'

'You mean, if the press finds a link between Wishart and Imogen?' I said.

He looked startled, but only for a second.

'Yes, that's precisely what I mean,' he said. 'What Imogen achieved in re-creating you was truly astounding. It was the greatest medical achievement of the twenty-first century and it would certainly be the greatest news story ever told. Naturally, with all this fuss over that imbecile Wishart, the media is on the hunt for the world's first clone and that has ramifications for me—for all of us.'

'Did you say "re-creating" me?'

'Yes!' He leaned across the table, his eyes bright with excitement. 'You are unique in the world, Dominic, the only one in whom the laws of nature have been reversed. The last frontier of the human condition—death—was defeated by what Imogen and I did. Think what a story that would be! Unfortunately, it's a story that would land me in prison and have very serious consequences for you.'

I looked at Mum. Her brow was furrowed into tight lines, her jaws tense. She was staring at me, pleading with her eyes. I felt the rage racing through me again, rage and disbelief. But somewhere in the middle of the rage was a still, calm centre, like the eye of a storm. He stood abruptly to deliver his final message.

'However, in many ways the fact that you now know the truth is a very positive thing. Now that you know who you are, you can truly be a part of it, you can really start to shape your destiny . . . '

'Michael . . . ' began Mum.

' . . . You're a very lucky young man. Your brother had a brilliant mind and you have an opportunity to capitalize on that gift. I hope you understand what I'm saying.'

'Yes, I do,' I said, holding his piercing gaze.

He'd made himself perfectly clear.

31

There'd been a change of plan, my father explained. We would now be leaving that evening, at six o'clock.

'I'd advise you to go and lie down, Carla,' he said, with a glance at Mum's empty wine glass. 'And, Dominic, you too will benefit from rest. We'll be leaving in approximately four hours' time, so I suggest we meet up at five thirty. I have some last-minute things to attend to. I shall be in my study if anyone needs me. Carla, could you send the nurse up to see me and I'll settle her bill.'

He left the room and I forced myself to smile at Mum's anxious face.

'So, that's it then,' I said cheerfully. 'We're really going.'

'Yes.' She smiled back. 'I think I will go and have a rest. It's going to be a long flight.'

I sat alone in the kitchen for a few moments, my head throbbing with tension. I'd made up my mind. There was no choice. But I knew that what I had to do now was just keep going—don't look back, don't think.

I went outside to the bench and found my rucksack. Giles's card and my mobile were still there, where I'd left them. I dug around to find my wallet and saw that the clothes I'd packed before were gone. And my money had been taken too. The wallet was empty, apart from a few coins. I looked in the compartment deep down in the back of the wallet. The Jiddy card was still there, so at least there was the possibility of getting cash, if I had time. The surprising thing was that the paints Imogen had given me were still there and so were the sketchbooks that I always kept tucked away in the zip compartment. I turned the box of paints over in my hands, remembering what she'd said about being an ally. Some ally!

I took the rucksack back to the summer lounge. The room was empty, my rumpled hospital bed, the scanner, and the drips standing silent in the sunshine. I found some clothes in a drawer and was just stuffing them into the rucksack when the door opened behind me. I spun round. It was the nurse, coming to collect her things.

She looked at my rucksack, hesitated a second, then smiled.

'It's always the last few bits and bobs that take the time,' she said. 'You take it easy, Dominic. Do as you're told and you'll be fine. I should have a sleep if I were you.'

'I will,' I said. 'Thanks for your help.'

'My pleasure,' she said. 'Good luck!'

She went, and a few moments later I heard the scrunch of her electrocar pulling away on the gravel at the side of the house. I finished stuffing the clothes into my rucksack, then went to the door to listen. If Mum had had her usual dose of wine, she'd be asleep all afternoon. The real problem was that my father's study was at the front of the house, facing down the long driveway to the security gates. So I'd have to take the long route round, leaving the property from the back and going across a couple of fields, skirting round till I reached the monorail.

I looked at my watch. It was almost half past two. I needed to get a move on. I slid the patio doors open, cursing the metallic dragging sound which seemed to rip across the still afternoon. I struggled the rucksack onto my back and tightened the straps, then took a firm hold of the crutches. I stared out at the wide emerald lawn. Just a bit of it to cross and then I'd reach the little copse of trees. Beyond the copse was a fairly steep slope towards the stream. Getting across that stream might be tricky, but it was at its narrowest around there and it was the only way out that didn't involve the three-metre perimeter wall.

I was shaking. If I started on this and was caught . . . I couldn't think about that. I just had to hope I'd be lucky and that no one would miss me until five thirty. I had three hours. I squeezed hard on the handgrips of the crutches and swung myself out onto the lawn. My heart was hammering, but I focused on the copse and got my rhythm going, swinging from crutches to my right foot again and again in long strides until I reached the shade of the trees.

I stopped under the oak tree, panting from the effort and from terror, and looked back at the house. Nothing moving. I turned back towards the trees and began making my way through to the slope on the other side. This wasn't so easy. The ground was rough and there were loads of tree roots. I was in such a panic about what I was doing that I was hurrying too much and once or twice the crutches slipped and I landed awkwardly on my right foot. I made myself slow down and place the crutches more carefully. If I did my ankle in, that would be the end of it.

I reached the slope and here I really did have to take it slowly. The ground fell more steeply towards the stream than I remembered. Swinging forwards wasn't an option. The best bet was to sit and bump my way down the slope on my bum. Carefully, on my heels, hands, and bum, I reached the edge of the stream. This was going to be more difficult than I'd reckoned too, because the stream was wider than I'd remembered. I'd have to wade across—I couldn't risk trying to swing myself across and maybe landing badly. I sat on the bank, took off my trainers, and rolled up my jeans. The dressing was still firmly stuck to my left calf, but it would just have to take its chance. If it

159

came off, it came off. It surely couldn't make much difference now.

I waded across the stream and, once on the other side, I was off our property. There was one field to cross and another to skirt round. I looked back at the house again. I'd have to be quick across the field so as to minimize chances of being seen, although it was only my bedroom, two of the guest rooms, and the bathrooms that looked out in this direction from the first floor. From the ground floor you couldn't see much of this field because of the wall and the trees.

I got quite a speed up across the field, although it was tiring doing the last bit because it went up a slight hill. I came to a stile and clambered over that, landing in the last field before the road. Just a short way along the road and I'd reach the monorail station.

Suddenly I heard the drumming of helicopter blades from behind me. There was no cover. All I could do was to throw myself to the ground, knowing it would be hopeless. Flying at that height he'd see me. I lay on the baked earth, listening to the thudding blades draw close. It was too late to run now, even with two good legs. I pressed myself into the dust as the thing drew overhead, trembling, feeling stupid and humiliated—how could I have thought he wouldn't have noticed, that he wouldn't be watching me every minute! Now I could feel the air vibrating above me, the thudding of the blades and the thudding of my heart.

And then it moved on, the sound fading in the direction of the New Town. I raised my head to make sure and saw the shining metal skimming away from me through the sky. I hauled myself to my feet and looked back across the field I'd crossed. In the distance, I could just make out the glint of my father's helicopter sitting where he'd left it at the end of our land. I stood, waiting for my heart to stop smashing at my ribcage. I looked at my watch. Five to three. I slotted my arms back into the crutches and started off again in the direction of the road.

When I got to the monorail, the platform was unusually full. I bought a ticket with the change I had left and wandered down the platform, sensing the growing fidgetiness around me. People were looking at their watches and sighing. Instinctively, I looked at the information board, which was blank. I thought of asking someone how long they had been waiting, but I didn't want to draw attention to myself. A woman standing just in front of me turned suddenly, saying, 'This is ridiculous!' and walked away. I wondered what to do. It was quarter past three. Usually, I walked to Pops's place—but it took about forty minutes, so it would be longer with the crutches, maybe an hour. On the other hand, I couldn't hang around here too long. I kept one eye on the platform entrance as I waited.

As the minutes dragged on I went to lean against the wall, still watching the entrance, feeling drained and miserable, a dull ache throbbing at my head. Perhaps this just wasn't meant to be. Perhaps I should go back. It might not be too late—I could be back just after four. If they hadn't noticed already, they need never know what I'd tried to do.

I thought of the terrible scenes there would be when it was discovered that I'd legged it again. Maybe Mum was right. Maybe it would be best to pretend to go along with everything he wanted and keep a little piece of myself that he didn't know about. Trick him, take advantage of his money and then get the hell out of it when I was eighteen. Only three years.

The people on the platform began to stir and mutter. I looked along the line and saw the distant silver nose of a train glinting in the sun. Only three years. And if I didn't go to Australia, would I ever see them again? What would happen to Mum if she lost another son?

The train was approaching fast, leaning as the line curved into the station. But he could do a lot of damage in three years. And I didn't want a little piece of myself. I wanted all of myself. The train's whine seared through my aching head as it began to slow. It slid to a halt. The button for the door was just in front of me. I stepped forward, pressed it, and got onto the crowded train.

The doors hissed and the whining noise built as the train moved off. Amongst the people who had got off the train and were now walking towards the exit, I thought I saw a familiar head. A neat blonde head, hair flicking as she took short, sharp steps. I couldn't be sure. I willed her to turn round, but she didn't. I pressed my face against the window but, as the train gathered speed, her head was masked by other bobbing heads, and gone.

32

I slumped onto a seat, trying to think calmly whether it could really have been Leanne Kelsey. The monorail station was only there to serve a small out-of-town retail park and if it *was* her, she surely couldn't have come here to shop. I remembered how Becky had panicked when Giles told her that Leanne had seen me. I remembered Giles standing in front of me, trying to get us away from her. Fear thundered around inside me and I willed the train to go faster. Only five minutes to the stop I needed! Thank God I wasn't at home. She could be walking up to the security gates now. But on the other hand, shouldn't she be in Brussels fronting news reports about Wishart's death sentence? Surely she should. And there must be loads of blonde women with that style of hair. I tried to convince myself. But by the time the train slowed, I knew that, either way, I was doing the right thing. This time I'd go somewhere where no one would find me.

As I got off the train, my head still throbbing, I was trying to plan things. I'd spent most of the money I had on the ticket, so I'd have to try and get some more cash with the Jiddy card, but I couldn't waste time on that now. The important thing was to get to Pops. I swung myself down the station ramp and hurried on down the tree-lined road towards him, desperate to see the familiar face of the house tucked away at the end of the long front garden that Pops used to fill with plants and flowers. The garden wasn't as good as it used to be, but sometimes we still worked on it together. On a good day he could tell me what was a weed

163

and what wasn't or show me how to encourage a sick plant. I wondered if he'd cope with being away from the house. Well, he'd just have to, because there was no way I could leave him behind on his own.

I rounded the corner and saw a lorry parked outside the house. A couple of big guys were carrying something across the lawn towards it. I read the words on the side of the lorry. And then I threw down the crutches and ran.

'Hey! Stop that!' I leapt over the front flowerbed and almost crashed into the two guys and the thing they were carrying. It was Pops's armchair.

'Stop it!' I yelled. 'Put it down! What are you doing?'

'House clearance. The old boy who lived here's gone, mate.'

'Put the chair down! Put it down, put it down!' I screamed.

I grabbed at the arm of the chair, with its patched material and lumpy stuffing. One of the guys tried to pull me off and I punched him hard in his flabby stomach. I heard a man shout behind me.

'Oi! Lunatic! Watch it, will yer?'

Still I clung to the stuffed armrest, screaming, kicking at the third guy who had run across from the lorry.

'Jeez! He's a nutter!' said one of them.

And then I heard a woman's voice. 'Leave him! Let him have the chair. It's his grandfather's!'

They let go of the chair and I fell into it, sobbing against the faded material that still smelt of him. I heard the woman's voice again and felt a hand on my shoulder.

'Dominic, it's me, Margi.'

'They didn't tell me,' I sobbed. 'They didn't tell me he was dead!'

'He isn't dead. Oh, Dominic, sweetheart, it's all right. Your grandfather's still alive.'

I looked up, not believing. Margi turned to the men.

'Would you be so kind as to bring the chair to my house, next door? The boy's had a shock. It seems he didn't know that his grandfather has moved.'

'Moved? Margi, what have they done with him?'

'He's gone to an assessment centre. Didn't your parents tell you?'

'NO!'

'Come on, come with me and I'll tell you all about it.'

'But they're taking his things!'

'Your father's already been to sort out the important things to keep.'

Of course he had. The invisible puppeteer again, sorting everybody out. I suddenly felt as if every drop of my life was draining away, sucking downwards out of me. My legs buckled and I let Margi lead me into her kitchen. One of the men brought Pops's chair and I sat on it.

'Your father said you were away visiting friends before you went abroad,' said Margi. 'That's right, isn't it? You're going to live abroad for a while?'

I shrugged. 'That's what he says.'

'Your father felt that your grandfather would be better off in a Home,' said Margi. 'I mean, I suppose that's for the best since he'll have no family around to keep an eye on him. I'm sorry, I had no idea that you didn't know what was happening. Apparently he has to be assessed to see what sort of Home he needs and then . . . well, I'm sure your parents will make sure he's in a comfortable place. They'll arrange everything for the best.'

I didn't answer. There was no answer to give.

'Come along, love,' she said. 'There's someone here to see you. He doesn't want to see you all upset, now does he?'

A heavy weight was plonked on my lap. I looked into the familiar ginger face of our one-eared cat, Caliban. He was purring, nudging his nose into my hand.

'He's glad to see you,' said Margi.

I caught her kind smile, wondered how much she understood about my family. Perhaps she knew things weren't as wonderful as they looked from the outside.

'Margi, I've got to get to Scotland. I can't tell you why, but I've got to. And I want to take Pops too if I can. But I don't know how to get there. I can be traced if I buy a ticket for rail or air travel and, believe me, my father will have me traced.'

'Have you traced?' She frowned. 'You mean, you're running away?'

'Yes,' I said.

'Oh, Dominic! Why?'

'My father wants to destroy me. You don't know what sort of man he is!'

'Well . . . ' She looked troubled. 'I know he's a difficult man, though it's not my place to say so. But he *is* your father. Surely it's best to try and talk things through.'

'Margi, I've tried. But he's done something so awful . . . I can't tell you what he's done.'

'It's that serious?'

'Yes.'

She sat on the arm of the chair, examining me with sad eyes.

'And you truly do need help?'

'Yes, Margi, yes! Why? Can you help me?'

'Only if you tell me *why* you want to run away.'

'I can't.'

'You can, Dominic. God knows, I've had four sons of my own. I can see it, I know you haven't had things easy, for all the money your parents have. But are you sure that running away is the right thing to do? It could just make the whole thing worse.'

'Margi, I . . . ' It was impossible to begin. How do you begin to tell someone something so huge?

'Has he hit you?' she asked gently.

'No.' It was the truth.

'So . . . it's worse than that? You know, if it's something the police should know about, I can't . . . '

'NO! No, Margi, it's . . . it's nothing you can imagine. Nothing like that.'

Her kind eyes swept over my face. 'What, then? Let me help you, Dominic.'

I took a deep breath. 'I don't think anyone can help me. And it's something you can't imagine because . . . because it's something that's never happened before. If anyone finds out about it my father could be in real trouble.'

I thought about this for the first time. He was still my father. And I didn't want him to go to prison. Or worse. I stood up.

'I'm sorry, Margi, I can't tell you.'

'Then I can't help you.' Her face was clouded-over, stern.

I nodded. 'Did the cat bring his basket with him?'

'Yes, they were delivered by your father's chauffeur.'

This was almost ridiculous. My father having the humanity to do the right thing by the cat. Or perhaps it was Mum's idea.

'Then I'll take him with me. Will you tell me where they took Pops? Do you know?'

'I'll write down the address, but you'll probably know it. It's the assessment centre in Circle Street. Dominic, please, please tell me what's wrong.'

I knew Circle Street. It was about ten minutes' walk. I looked at my watch and saw that it was nearly half-past four, which meant the best I could hope for was that I had an hour before my father discovered I was gone. Maybe Pops could come with me, maybe he couldn't. But I knew I couldn't leave without saying goodbye.

'Margi, I haven't much time. The cat basket, please?'

She found the basket and I scooped Caliban up and stuffed him in. He wasn't that pleased about it, but then he always did have a good line in looking huffy. I poked the last twitch of tail in and fastened the catches.

We got the crutches and I tried to see if I could walk and carry the basket. Even though my left leg was aching from my dash across the lawn, I managed a few paces using just one crutch on the left side and carrying the cat basket in my right hand. But I knew I couldn't keep this up all the way to Circle Street.

'Dominic, this is silly!' cried Margi as I tottered sideways and nearly fell. I had to let go of the basket and Caliban yowled like a werewolf as it hit the ground.

'I'll have to leave him!' I said.

I didn't even want to look at him a last time. I couldn't.

'*Promise* me you'll look after him, Margi!'

'Of course I will, but . . . ' She caught my arm, held on to me, made me look into her worried face.

'He's done something so wrong that you can't tell me?'

'No, it's not wrong . . . I can't say it's *wrong*, because if he hadn't done it I wouldn't be here, I wouldn't be alive. And it wasn't his fault that Nick died . . . '

'Who's Nick?'

'He was my brother . . . ' I found that I was crying again. And then it all rushed out . . . 'He was my brother and he died and no one could bear it, so my father had him cloned to make me.'

I wiped my eyes and found her face. Her expression told me immediately that I should have kept my mouth shut. Horror, revulsion.

'Cloned?' She stared at me.

'Yes. My life has never been my own, and if I go with my father it never will be. He only ever wanted me to replace Nick.'

168

'Oh God!' she breathed. 'Oh God, Dominic, I don't know what to do.'

'Neither do I,' I said. 'I'm just doing what feels right.'

And I swung off down the path, leaving her standing in shock at this terrible thing I should never have told her. I tried not to hear Caliban's angry yowling, tried not to think about the expression on Margi's face as I set off to find Pops.

33

The assessment centre was a modern building that had been designed to look like a cosy huddle of bungalows. The waft of disinfectant hit you as soon as the automatic doors slid open. I had a good look round the reception area. At first I thought there was no one at the desk and I'd be able to get past undetected, although I hadn't got a clue where to look for Pops. Then a hassled-looking woman with grey curls and glasses appeared through a swing door, which bashed behind her.

'Yes?' she snapped.

Just what I needed. She glared at me over the top of her glasses as she took up guard behind the desk.

'Yes? Can I help you?'

A charm offensive was the only way to go. It usually worked with rude old bats.

'I'm terribly sorry to bother you,' I smiled. 'I've come to see my grandfather. He's . . . '

'Appointment?' said the bat.

'Sorry?'

'Visiting by appointment only. Do you have one?'

'No, but . . . '

'Visiting by appointment only. We find it's best to keep distractions to a minimum while they're being assessed. Once they've been assessed and placed in the appropriate unit, a visiting plan will be created in consultation with the unit director, the nominated carer, and other key staff.'

I wanted to scream at her but I knew I had to keep calm.

'Could I make an appointment?' I asked.

'When for?'

'For now.'

The eyes in her leathery face narrowed.

'Are you trying to be clever?'

'No, I'm trying to see my grandfather. He's not your property, you know!'

I felt the anger well up. Anger at her. At myself for blowing it. At everything.

'Out!' yelled the old bat. 'Unaccompanied minors are not permitted to . . . '

Another voice cut in and I turned to see Margi behind me. My heart began to thud painfully. I searched her face, trying to see what she would do, if she was going to betray me. One word from her and it was all over. She was avoiding my gaze. She looked stern, determined.

'He isn't unaccompanied,' she told the woman. 'My name's Margaret Thompson. I have an appointment to see this young man's grandfather. He can come with me. That *is* permitted, isn't it? Two visitors are allowed, I believe.'

The woman consulted a diary, then thrust it towards Margi and slapped down a pen.

'Sign here,' she said.

Margi signed, then grabbed my arm and led me down one of the squeaky-clean corridors. Once we were out of sight of reception, she stopped, turned to face me.

'Look,' she whispered, her voice shaking, 'I don't know whether I'm doing the right thing or not, but I understand the danger you're in. We've had *nothing but* talk of this business on the news lately, and now there's to be an execution, God help us! I'll keep what you told me to myself. And I'll help you—for your sake, your mother's, and grandfather's . . . '

'Oh, Margi . . . '

'But there are strings attached. First—I need to know

171

that there's someone to look after you, wherever you're going. Especially if you're serious about taking your grandfather with you.'

'Yes, Margi, there is! They're friends of my brother's, the best friends anyone could have . . . '

'What are their names?'

'Giles and Becky . . . '

'And does your mother know these people?'

'Yes. She knows them both, she'd trust them, I know she would.'

'So I can tell her you'll be with them? You'll be safe?'

I hesitated. 'Yes, but . . . my father mustn't find out.'

'He won't hear it from me,' she said. 'The other thing is, I want you to let me know, wherever you end up, that you're safe. Will you do that?'

'Of course . . . '

'All right then, if it's Scotland you want, my son Joe can get you there. My boys have a business transporting medical supplies. They have light aircraft going up and down all the time. Joe's outside waiting with an electrocar. So if you're still sure after you've seen your grandfather, there is a way.'

'Oh, Margi, thank you! I'll repay you when I can earn some money. You don't know how important this is . . . '

'Now don't get too excited,' she said. 'I saw your grandfather yesterday. You may notice a change.'

She led me down a corridor and through a door into a lounge with a blaring screen at one end. In front of the screen was a semi-circle of chairs containing old people. As we walked past them I felt like a trespasser, as if I shouldn't be there to notice that their skin was crêpe-paper thin, their eyes—those of them that were open—staring straight ahead while the mindless game-show pumped jarring noises and colours at them. I shivered and looked around for Pops. He was by himself at the other end of the

172

room, staring out of a window. He didn't look up as Margi and I approached.

'Pops!' I yelled out to him and he turned his head towards me. His eyes were dead, like the other ghosts. And then suddenly a light seemed to flick on.

'Some of these people are mad!' he said. 'And they're all awfully old. I wouldn't want to stay here!'

'Pops!' I said. 'Pops, do you know who I am?'

He frowned. 'Look like a nice chap. Can't place you.'

Margi sighed. 'He seems to come and go. I don't think this is like . . . well, it's not like those poor souls that really have Alzheimer's, is it? I don't know, I just don't . . . '

Suddenly, Pops was looking sad.

'It's my own fault,' he said. 'Someone wanted to find out about Dominic and I tried to stop it. I tried to stop it but I couldn't! He died, you know. It's my own fault they put me here.'

I looked into his faded eyes. Poor old Pops, it *was* him who had hidden the photo album that I'd found in the attic. He'd known all along. Was that what sent him mad, scrambled his thoughts? The horror of it?

I took his hand. 'It's all right, Pops, I understand. I know exactly what you mean. It's not your fault. You've done nothing wrong and you don't have to stay here. Would you like to come with me?'

He smiled. 'Yes. I know who you are.'

'Do you?' I said. 'Do you really?'

'You're my grandson. The younger one.'

'Yes, Pops, yes!' I happened to glance down at my watch as he squeezed my hand. Nearly half past five. Oh, God!

'Come with me, Pops. You don't want to stay here.'

'Certainly don't!' he said.

We found the room he'd been allocated, and in it the small suitcase which he hadn't unpacked.

173

'We'll never get this past reception!' I said. 'It'll give the game away.'

'I've got a shopping bag in my handbag,' said Margi. 'Put the important things in that. They'll never notice.'

'There's no other way out?' I asked.

'I wouldn't risk it—we wouldn't want to set off an alarm,' said Margi.

So I packed Pops's radio, slippers, and a change of clothes into the carrier bag and the three of us went back to the old bat in reception.

'Mr Richardson's just coming out for a little walk around the park with his grandson,' explained Margi.

The woman frowned. Obviously people were expected to stay put.

'You're sure you want to go with these people?' she asked Pops. 'Do you know who they are?'

Pops looked doubtful for a second, then nodded. 'She's Margi from next door.'

'Your neighbour, yes. And who's this?'

'That's my grandson. The younger one.'

She looked annoyed, but she'd run out of ammunition. 'Very well,' she said. 'You may go, but bear in mind that all residents must be in the dining room for supper at six o'clock sharp.'

Pops fixed her with a glare that would have put Caliban to shame. As we reached the door I turned and smiled sweetly at her. 'I do hope your personality disorder is curable,' I said.

Margi tutted and shoved me out along the path towards the waiting electrocar.

A few paces down the street was a rubbish bin. I had something to put in it, the final thing I could do to put my father off the scent, something I should have thought of before I started all this. I pulled my mobile out of my pocket and dumped it in the bin. If he put a trace on it, which he certainly would, he might just reach it before it got to the city recyc plant.

As I opened the electrocar door to help Pops into the back seat, I saw the cat basket, with Caliban's sulking face pressed up against the bars. He spat ungratefully as I poked a finger through to stroke his head.

Margi's son Joe appeared beside me, a round guy with a beard. I'd seen him before, helping Margi in her garden. 'He's been in the wars, then,' he said. 'Never seen a one-eared cat before.'

'Yeah, he's a one-off,' I said. 'Thanks for bringing him!'

'Not that I didn't want him,' said Margi. 'In fact, I've grown rather attached to him. But he belongs with you.'

We got Pops safely installed in the back next to Caliban and I jumped in the front. Margi said she'd walk home so as to let us get on our way quickly.

'Thanks for everything, Margi,' I said.

'You can thank me by taking care of yourself,' she said. 'And by doing the right thing. I'm sure you will.'

'I'll try.'

As Joe pulled away, a folded newspaper slid along the dashboard shelf. I caught it and glanced at the headline. 'All I ever wanted was a perfect family.' There was a picture of a pretty woman. I recognized the face. It was the woman for whom Wishart had tried to clone a baby, the ex-model who wanted a little girl so that her looks would live on. I scanned the story. It was the woman's 'true story', a load of tosh about how she'd always wanted a perfect family and it was her right to have a perfect child if she wanted. Wishart had offered it and she could afford to pay. The three boys she already had were also pictured, looking a bit glum.

The perfect family. The perfect child! I began to laugh and, once it started, like pebbles rolling down a hill, my laugh couldn't stop.

'Steady on, mate,' grinned Joe. 'You'll do yourself a mischief!'

'I'm sorry,' I spluttered.

'Well, what I say about life,' said Joe, ' . . . is that you've got to laugh. Keep yourself cheerful. Right, let's go to Scotland!'

Two hours later our little plane took off, carrying what remained of my family. The one-eared cat, the clone, and the mad old man.

34

We found a bench in a corner of the busy flights concourse at Link 73. There were a dozen Links in Scotland, a fact that I hadn't even considered. When I'd phoned Giles from the Link in Surrey and given him the number of the one we were due to land at in Scotland, I'd never even heard of the place. But we'd been lucky. Although this wasn't the closest Link to where Giles and Becky were staying, it was the closest one with an airport. It was three hours by electrocar and Giles said he could hire one from the nearby village. So he should be with us soon. I fidgeted, standing guard over Pops while he dozed.

Joe was making his way across the lounge, carrying a tray, dodging the scurrying passengers and their trolleys, some transferring from air to rail, some looking for electrocar hire or taxis. This Link was on the edge of a big city, apparently. I sat down next to Pops, aware of the sheet glass walls that formed our little corner. Beyond those walls, darkness. And we were lit up as though we were in a shop window.

Joe arrived, grinning. 'I've had to sell the plane to buy these sandwiches! Hope they're good!'

'Thanks, Joe. I'm sorry, I haven't any . . . '

'Nah, nah, I didn't say it for that. Tuck in!'

He handed me sandwiches and coffee. We looked to see if Pops would like anything, but he was still dozing. Caliban was hunched in his basket, subdued. I posted some ham from my sandwich through the bars. He glared as if I was trying to poison him.

'Thing is, though,' said Joe, 'have you got . . . I mean, are you all right for . . . '

'Oh yes, money's no problem,' I said. 'I'll get some soon.'

This sounded a bit limp, but it was the best I could do. I was trying not to think about how we could actually survive with no money. I'd get a job as soon as I could. And there was something else worrying me. Joe was a chatty sort of guy, friendly, interested in people. I'd thanked him for helping me and told him he needn't hang around until Giles arrived, but he'd insisted. Now I knew I had to say something. A woman with a pushchair was heading our way and Joe stood, making room for her to sit.

'The thing is, Joe,' I said, 'it's really important that no one knows I'm here.'

'Take it as read, mate.' He smiled and slurped his coffee.

'No, I mean, really, really important . . . '

For a second I thought he looked hurt, but then he said, 'My mum said you needed help. That's good enough for me. I'll keep my mouth shut.'

'Thanks,' I said, feeling bad that I'd said anything.

The woman arrived and parked her pushchair. It was a very wide one. I budged up as she flumped onto the bench with a sigh. I looked at the two toddlers sitting in the pushchair and my heart skipped a beat. Two little boys with exactly the same face. One just staring at me, the other smiling shyly.

'Twins!' cried Joe, squatting in front of the pushchair. 'Hello, fellas! Aren't they gorgeous?' He turned to the mother with a grin.

'Double trouble!' she said. 'But yes, they are gorgeous.'

Both twins looked at Joe and both smiled. Identical smiles. Joe chattered on, asking their names and ages; I

178

just stared at them. Suddenly, I remembered something the priest had said on the news item I'd seen back in Cambridge. Biologically, a clone is no different to a twin, or something like that. Did that mean that Nick and I were sort of twins? The little boys were looking at each other now. What was it like to see your own face looking back at you? They had pale red curls and freckles. Even the freckles were in the same places, or it looked as if they were. One of them, the one who'd smiled at me before, caught me staring and gazed back, seeming to examine every last detail in my face.

'You know,' said their mother, 'what with all that's going on in the news, people keep asking me if they're clones!' She laughed. 'I say, ''No, they're jolly well not, they're natural!'' '

'And quite different, I bet,' said Joe.

'Oh, yes, they've both got their personalities!'

I jumped up, brushing past Joe.

'All right, mate?' he asked.

'Just going for a walk,' I managed to say, hoping he hadn't seen my face. That was the point, I thought bitterly, those two little boys were 'natural'. I wasn't. For the sake of looking as if I was going somewhere, I walked against the crowd of people sweeping across the concourse. Hurrying, chattering, normal people. The glare of light flooded everything and noise was pumping from huge advertising screens, gambling units, and TV monitors. I found myself looking at people, their bodies, their faces. Staring at them. Wide hips, slim legs, bald heads, big noses . . . happy faces, haunted faces, broken faces. Each person a random jumble of genes, weathered by a random jumble of experiences. What would happen if the world ever stopped being random? What would it mean?

My head ached as I looked up to see a TV screen punch the I-dent of the EuroNews at me and then—almost as if

she'd heard my question and had come to answer it—
Imogen's face appeared on the screen. I pressed forward in
the crowd, trying to hear what she was saying. But the
noise of people around me was so loud, I couldn't hear. I
watched her mouth, trying to lip-read. She looked serious,
her beautiful, intelligent eyes concentrating on the person
questioning her. I searched for any hint of unease in her
face. The interviewer with her, one of the top anchormen
on TV news, looked serious too. A chill ran through me.
Had they found out? Please God, don't let it be that!

'Tell you who I'd clone,' said a voice nearby. 'I'd clone
the computer operator that does my wages. Double my
salary in one go!'

'I'd clone anyone but the wife!' yelled someone else.
They all laughed.

I tried to press forward again. Imogen, what are you
saying? I felt a hand on my shoulder and nearly screamed
out loud. I turned and saw Giles's worried face. He clapped
me round the shoulders and managed a tight smile.

'Thank God you're here!' I whispered. 'What's
happening?'

He looked at the screen. 'It's OK, I think. Just a routine
interview. Come on, let's get out of here.'

We pushed through the crowds, back to our corner of
the concourse. Pops was now awake, eating his sandwich
and making faces at the twins, who were giggling
hysterically at him. Joe seemed to be getting on quite well
with their mother.

'A-HA!' Pops jumped up when he saw Giles. 'Don't I
know you?'

'Yes. Hello, Mr Richardson,' said Giles. 'Giles Nickalls.
We met a long time ago.'

'Yes, quite so,' said Pops. His eyes wandered to me
doubtfully and back to Giles. 'Long time ago, as you say.'

They shook hands and I could tell that Pops did

remember Giles really. I wondered how much of Pops's memory loss was real and how much was pretend and how much of the pretend, over the years, had become real.

'I'll keep my promise,' said Joe, shaking my hand as Giles picked up the cat basket.

'I know. Thanks for everything. Have a good trip home,' I said.

And then Giles, Pops, a basket full of sulking fur, and I set off for the car park to find the electrocar. Getting out of the huge Link complex took some time because of the traffic, but then we were heading out into open country. The car became a dark cocoon as we left the blazing lights of the Link, and I lay down on the back seat and tried to sleep. But my mind was full of fear. I thought of that sea of people in the concourse and the great tide of people that had swept through life since it all began. As exhaustion pulled me down into sleep, I remember thinking that I'd rather be any of them, any one of them, than be me.

35

I was lolling against a window and as I opened my eyes I saw that we were moving through mist, the faint whine of the electrocar the only noise in the dense quiet. I stretched my cramped legs.

'Well, you two have been great company,' said Giles from the driver's seat. 'The cat and I have had a good chat about religion and politics, though.'

I leaned forward and saw that Pops was sleeping.

'We're nearly there,' added Giles.

'How can you tell?' I said, staring out at the dark shapes moving behind the milky gauze.

'I think we're just coming up to the valley where the cottage is,' said Giles. 'It's really very pretty when you can see it.'

I opened the window and sniffed.

'Giles, can we stop?' I said.

'What for?'

'Please!'

He pulled over and I stepped out into air scented with earthy vegetation and water, like nothing I'd ever smelt or breathed before. I sucked in lungfuls. You could hear water running over rocks out there, and beyond that there was something else. I looked up and saw pale grey peaks carved above the mist.

'The mountains!' I said, as Giles came to stand beside me. 'They're so . . . high!'

'There are paths,' he said. 'You can climb them.'

As we stood listening, the mist began slowly to lift, to

show sheep nibbling the grass and shaggy, horned cattle nodding their ginger heads and bellowing clouds of breath into the morning.

'We're further up the road than I thought,' said Giles. 'If this lot lifts we should be able to see the lake in a while.'

We waited and gradually things became clear. Ahead of us, the mist was being sucked away from the dark, silky surface of a lake. It floated upwards across the purple-grey shoulders of the mountains.

'We didn't know what to do, you know,' said Giles, 'when your father took you. Imogen said it was for the best, that he would be the best one to protect you, with all his power and money. And then afterwards, when we got home, Becky said we should come here as planned, that you'd let us know if you needed us.'

'Thanks, Giles,' I said.

'I take it things didn't work out,' he said.

'I'll tell you about it when we get home,' I said. I didn't want to spoil this moment with thoughts of my father. My old life was behind me now, far away. We watched the last puffs of mist clear the tops of the mountains and take off into pale blue sky.

'It's going to be a lovely day,' said Giles. And then he pointed towards a white cottage on the opposite shore of the lake. 'That's where we're headed. And a few kilometres further down on this side is the village, so we're not totally isolated.' He took in a huge breath of air. 'God, I'm looking forward to my breakfast!'

'Yeah,' I said. 'Bacon and eggs! I'm starving!'

'Kippers!' he said, getting back into the car. 'Don't talk to me about bacon and eggs—you're in Scotland! You're having kippers!'

'Kippers?' said Pops. 'Oh, good!'

We drove round the lake. I couldn't take my eyes off the mountains hugging up along the opposite shore, perfectly replicated upside-down in the glass-flat water. To the other side of us was a forest of dark pines from which rivulets of water seeped, trickling under or over the road to feed the lake.

'You can never get enough of this landscape,' said Giles. 'And it's always changing. It has its own moods.'

We left the shade of the pines as the shore curved round and now, with the sun behind us, we were heading towards the mountains. It was below them that the white cottage could just be seen in amongst some trees.

At last we turned off the road and crunched down a driveway. At the end, facing away from us and towards the lake, was the cottage, an overgrown lawn surrounding it. As the car came to a halt, I blinked in the sunlight and stared across the glittering water, feeling a tightening in my chest. Remember this, I thought. Remember it and keep it forever.

'There are some stones for a campfire down by the shore,' said Giles as we got out of the car. 'We could cook outside.'

The front door of the cottage swung open, and there was Becky, looking worried and pleased.

'Thank God you're safe! What happened?' she said.

I took a few steps towards her and saw the glint of tears in her eyes.

'Long story.'

She nodded. She opened her arms and the next thing I knew we were wrapped together and I felt the heave of her chest as she stifled a sob, felt the wetness on her cheek as she kissed me. Suddenly she turned away to help Pops out of the electrocar.

'Mr Richardson! How lovely! It's such a relief to see you, both of you . . . ' She saw and heard the cat basket which Giles was taking out from the back seat, 'or should I say, all three of you!'

184

We shut Caliban in the cottage with a dirt box and a tin of tuna and let him settle in private, and then Giles and Becky carried an armchair down to the lakeside for Pops.

I built the fire, choosing smooth grey rocks and arranging them in a circle. There was some dry wood in the cottage and Becky brought a shelf from the oven and laid it over the stone circle. Soon the crackling of fire and the hissing of the kippers was mingling with the sound of the lake nibbling at the shore.

'He took me home and got a nurse in to keep me drugged up,' I said. 'They said it was because I had to keep still—they were worried about blood clots moving. I suppose he didn't want to risk me doing a runner again before he could get me to Australia.'

I rolled up my jeans and examined the dressing. Surely it could come off now. I pulled at a corner of the tape and peeled the neat square of white off my calf. I wasn't really surprised at what I saw.

'Look.' I stretched out my leg for them to see. There was just a tiny pale mark.

'That must be a stitch mark—from when they went in to get the bullet out,' said Becky. 'It looks fine.'

'I reckon it's been fine for a week or more. I reckon the pain in my legs was only because I'd been lying in bed so long.'

'For God's sake,' cried Becky. 'The man's not sane!'

'Mum was just going along with what he wanted because she's frightened. She thinks the media will eat me alive if they find me.'

I looked at Pops, wondering how much of this he was taking in. He was leaning over the side of his armchair, twiddling a stick in the sand.

'So what was your father's plan for the long term?' asked Giles.

185

'New identities in Australia. Pops shoved into a home for mad old people.'

The stick fell still in Pops's speckled hand and he stared out across the lake, seemingly lost in thought. Lost somewhere, anyway.

'He spelled it out for me,' I said. 'I'm expected to make the most of the opportunity I've been given.'

'What does he mean by that?' asked Becky.

I caught the look she threw at Giles. They knew.

'The opportunity of living again. Because I've been brought back from the dead. He believed he could control the one thing that no one has ever been able to control—the fact that we all die in the end. He ordered it done. He paid for a dead son to live again.'

'But surely . . . ' began Giles.

'It's what he wants to believe,' I said. 'That I am Nick.'

'And your mother?' asked Becky.

'I think she's always understood who I am and who he is. That's why she drinks. She drinks instead of fighting. I'm on my own.'

Giles touched a hand to my shoulder. He leaned forward and fiddled with the fish.

'So, anyway, I don't want to sponge off you,' I said. 'I'll get a job as soon as I can. Are there any farms or hotels—places where I could work for cash?'

Becky shook her head. 'We'll sort something out about money—don't worry about it yet. It's best if you stay put here for the moment, just in case.'

Of course she was right. You can't just escape from your crazy father, kidnap an old man and expect no one to notice. They would be looking for me. Or would they? Something had just occurred to me.

'The police won't come after me,' I said. 'My father wouldn't let it come to that, he wouldn't want to draw attention to us. If anyone's going to find me, he'll want to make sure it's him.'

'We should be pretty safe here,' said Giles. 'Our neighbour back in Cambridge, who owns the cottage, is the only one who knows where we are. You did call her, didn't you, Becks?'

Becky nodded. 'I called her this morning, just before you arrived, to ask her not to say anything to anyone. We'll just lie low until the fuss over Wishart has died down. It'll be OK.'

I stirred the fire beneath the fish as I thought about who knew I was here, or who could find out. Only Margi and Joe knew that I was in Scotland. My father would ask Margi if she'd seen me, that was for sure, and if the old bat at the assessment centre said she'd seen us together . . .

'Scotland's a big country, though, isn't it?' I said.

'It is,' said Becky. 'And no one comes to the cottage except the postman. Try not to worry.'

'The other thing is,' I said, 'I don't know if it's anything, really, but I saw someone who could have been Leanne Kelsey when I was getting on the monorail at the station near home. I only got a really quick glimpse. She had the same sort of haircut, but . . . I don't know.'

'When was this?' asked Giles.

'Yesterday afternoon.'

He shot a questioning look at Becky. She frowned. 'She'd have been in Brussels yesterday, reporting on the Wishart sentence. It couldn't have been her, I'm certain.'

'Needs a lot of work,' said Pops.

'What does, Pops?' I asked.

'The garden. Flowerbeds.' He gestured towards the cottage. 'In a mess. I'll get going on them.'

'There are some tools in the shed, Mr Richardson, if you'd really like to have a go,' said Becky.

She smiled and handed Pops a plate of kippers and

brown bread and butter. He beamed at her and took the plate excitedly.

'To put you in the picture,' said Giles, 'our neighbour in Cambridge wants to sell this place. Becks and I might buy it. This is a sort of trial holiday to see if we like it here.'

'If you do buy it, you'll need some help knocking it into shape,' I said.

Giles grinned. 'There you go then, you can work for your keep!'

I looked up at the mountains, which were brightening into warmer colours under the gentle brush of sunlight. And for the first time since I'd grabbed my grandfather and my cat and run, I began to feel that I'd done the right thing.

36

Later that morning I found myself a boulder down by the lake. I wanted to try some sketches of the way the mountains were reflected in the water. I ran upstairs to my tiny, beamed bedroom, grabbed my sketchbook and some pencils and was on my way back past the kitchen when I heard Giles and Becky talking.

I stopped, shivering slightly in the dark passageway and trying to quieten my breathing as I listened to Becky's voice.

'If she'd been in Brussels yesterday, she'd have filed a report. And there's no report, at least not that I can find on the Net. So where the hell was she?'

They were talking about Leanne Kelsey. Must be.

'She's one of the top reporters working on the Wishart case,' continued Becky. 'She should have been there to hear the sentence, she should have made a report. Unless there was something else that interested her more. What if the break-in at Imogen's lab *was* something to do with Leanne? What if she's on to Dominic? Her next step would have been to go after him at home. So it *could* have been her at the monorail station . . .'

'OK, let's suppose it was Leanne,' said Giles, 'and let's suppose they go ahead and execute Wishart. Surely that would stop her. She wouldn't want to pursue any story that could incriminate Imogen, knowing that this would lead to the execution of one of the most respected research scientists in the world. Where's the public justice in that?'

'Oh, Giles, you're so naive! Leanne's not interested in

justice. Dom's story is worth billions in newspaper sales alone! Why would she care about Imogen? Or about Dom? If she breaks this story she's made for the rest of her life!'

'All right, then,' said Giles, 'even if it was her at the monorail station, she's got no way of tracing Dom, because even his parents don't know where he is. As you said, we'll just lie low and see how the Wishart case pans out. I hate myself for thinking this, but the sooner they execute him, the safer Dom will be. Dead men don't talk.'

'That's one way of looking at it,' said Becky. 'Do you think we should try and contact Carla? We've got her son and her father and she must be worried sick.'

'Yes, but how do we get hold of Carla without Michael noticing? We'll ask Dom what he wants to do. Give him a while to settle, though. Try not to worry, Becks. Come here.'

'Hmmm,' she murmured. 'Love you, Dr Nickalls.'

Then there was silence and it felt as if it was time for me to go. Then Giles said, 'Umm . . . is that cat *supposed* to be in the fridge?'

'Oh no!' she laughed. 'He's got your ham!'

'*My* ham? How d'you know it's *mine*?'

'Shooo!' she shrieked.

And I scarpered before I could be caught too. I went to sit on my boulder and a few moments later Becky wandered down to join me.

'Good landscape for drawing.' She squinted into the sun.

'Hmm.' I put down the sketchbook. I couldn't concentrate anyway. 'Becky, last night when I was at the Link waiting for Giles, I saw on one of the screens . . . there was an interview with Imogen, but I couldn't hear what they were saying. Did you see it? Was it anything to do with cloning?'

'Yes, I did see it. Cloning wasn't even mentioned. She

was talking about a new discovery she and her team have made . . . '

'About cancer?'

'Yes. You knew about it?'

'Sort of. So . . . she's really famous for all that stuff, isn't she? So if anyone tried to accuse her of cloning me, they'd have to be *so* sure they could prove it.'

'Yes, they would.'

'Do you think Leanne will find me?'

She gave me a deep look and for a moment I thought she'd guessed that I'd been listening to her and Giles. Then she jumped up. 'No, I don't think so. And I think *you* should stop thinking, Dom. Take some time off. Is the leg feeling up to a bit of a walk? I'll show you the path that leads up towards those mountains, if you like.'

I looked up at her smile and noticed again her delicate jawline and cheek bones, the bright energy in her eyes. I could see why Nick had loved her. I wondered if I'd ever have anyone like this to love me.

'OK,' I said.

So she took me on my first walk. It nearly bust my lungs open and my legs ached when we got back, but that didn't matter. I'd never been to a place like this before. Whenever we'd been away with my father, he'd chosen white sandy islands in the middle of an azure sea or some expensive hotel that could be anywhere. I'd never been high up in a place I'd climbed to myself. And as Becky and I walked, the horizon changed, showing us summits beyond sight of where we began.

We stopped to sit on a shoulder of grass high above the lake.

'Your leg OK?' asked Becky.

'Yeah, it's going to be,' I said. 'The walking will do it good.'

I looked at the incredible sweep and plunge of landscape

191

all around me. I could almost imagine myself as part of it, like one of the rocks or trees that grew out of it. Absurdly, I remembered something from one of my science lessons: 'All living things are made up of the same basic ingredients . . . ' What were they? Was it water, carbon, and nitrogen? Which meant that I was a living thing made from the same stuff as the rest of the planet. I hadn't thought of that before.

'I wonder if Simeon meant to kill me,' I said. 'It would be best for him and Imogen if I was out of the way.'

'I'm not going to tell you you're wrong,' said Becky. 'I believe that Simeon would do almost anything to protect Imogen. And he's temperamental, unpredictable, I know that. But it's a big step to say he meant to kill you. I think he just wanted to frighten all of us.'

'Well, he needn't worry. I'm not in a hurry to see him or her again.'

'Did it help, talking to her?' said Becky.

I shrugged. I didn't really want to talk about Imogen, even to Becky. And before I realized I was going to do it, I blurted out a question of my own. A question that no one had ever really answered. Perhaps it couldn't be answered.

'What was Nick really like?'

We sat in silence for a few seconds and I didn't look at her. I heard her sigh.

'I guess what you want to know is—was he really so perfect?' she said.

I looked at her and, again, her gaze back was searching deep into me.

'Yes,' I said, 'I suppose that *is* what I need to know. Is that awful?'

'No, it's not awful. I don't know if I'm the person to ask, though, because I was . . . I was so much in love with him. I think . . . he wasn't as strong as you. He didn't have to be. He never had to fight, not on his own behalf, anyway, because everything came so easily to him. That didn't make him a bad person, but it meant that sometimes he didn't . . . he didn't quite understand other people's struggles—or their weaknesses. And just between you and me . . . he could be quite selfish sometimes.' She smiled. 'Unlike you.'

Her words were buzzing in my head. 'I was so much in love with him.'

'He was so lucky to have you,' I said. And then I wished I hadn't said it, because her face reddened and she turned away. I felt I'd done something terrible, but I didn't know how to undo it.

'Becky . . .'

I saw the tears in her eyes and, without thinking, I moved in towards her, hugged her head onto my shoulder, rested my cheek and then my lips against her hair.

I felt her tense up. She drew away, one hand pushing gently at my shoulder, the other wiping her eyes. And then I knew I'd done something terrible.

'I'm sorry,' I choked.

'It's OK, Dom,' she sniffed, 'I'm sorry too.' She threw back her head and smiled sadly. 'It's weird, isn't it? Nobody else in the world, ever, has been in this situation before. It's like suddenly being snatched out of the life you have now and taken back sixteen years. Being round you wrong-foots me sometimes because there are moments when I remember so clearly what it was like to be eighteen and in love. It's silly of me, because I know you're not him and I certainly know I'm not eighteen any more! And I love Giles more than anything and . . .'

She hugged her knees towards her and stared out at the landscape. 'I think it's just . . . remembering being young. That time when anything and everything was possible.'

She reached out to touch me, made me look at her.

'I'm flattered that . . . that you're fond of me. But you've got it all to look forward to, Dom. Girlfriends.'

'Have I?' My face burned. Truth was, I'd never been able to talk to girls the way I wanted to. Not like I could talk to Becky.

'Yes. And it'll be wonderful,' she said.

'What do you think Nick would have done, if he had lived?' I asked in a wobbly voice. It was better if we talked about him, not me.

'I think he'd have wanted to do something in the Third World or teaching, campaigning, politics, perhaps. Your father wanted him at Gordon's Pharmaceuticals, of course.'

'Who would have won?'

She looked at me. 'Unanswerable question.'

'My life's full of them,' I said. 'Except—one question I can answer. *I'm* not going to work for my father. Way things are going, we'll probably never speak to each other again.'

'You're a brave man, you know, to run away from him twice.' She laughed.

'Brave or stupid.' I grinned. I jumped up and gave her my hand to help her up. She took it and I pulled her to her feet and for a moment we held hands.

Then we headed for home, down through the warmth that was seeping out of the rock. The rest of the world seemed far away, and no matter what happened there, it felt as though it could never reach here or touch these mountains that had been thrown up out of the earth and carved by ice, water, and wind through millions of years. The mountains were safe and strong and impenetrable. And, as Becky said, I had everything to look forward to.

37

Every day I climbed higher into the mountains, looking down on the cottage that had so quickly come to feel like home. Becky and Giles had decided to buy it and we were spending most mornings working at clearing, cleaning, and planning the refurbishments. Pops was doing amazing things with the garden. He'd discovered an overgrown herb plot and was determined to reinstate it to its former glory, clearing the choking weeds away and nursing the plants back to health. I'd kept my promise to Margi. I'd written a postcard saying, 'Safe. D, P, and C.' and given it to our postman.

The afternoons were my exploring times and I'd take my sketchbook and climb up the path through the pinewoods behind the cottage. The path led towards the sound of water hurtling over rocks on its race down to the lake and, just at the point where your legs began to ache from the climb, the trees ended and the path ran parallel with the river for a while before swinging away, up towards the higher peaks. My legs were getting stronger and as the days passed I pushed further up into the lonely, secret landscape.

I was beginning to steer myself in the direction I wanted to go. I was also beginning to understand how far there was to travel and how much I wanted to make that journey. I began to look, really look for the first time, at the things I was trying to paint and draw, and the more I looked at the mountains, the more they taught me about the colours and moods they wore, about shadow and light, distance and perspective.

The trouble was, I was running out of stuff. I needed more colours, different materials and brushes, and I was getting through so much paper. What I needed, of course, was money and I couldn't see a way of getting any—not for a while. And then, one morning when rain was slanting at the cottage windows and the lake was being whipped into little choppy waves, I hit upon the idea of using Becky's computer, if she'd let me, to work on an idea for a series of cards based on my landscape sketches. She spent a lot of time working on the laptop nowadays, but perhaps I could borrow it sometimes in the evening.

I found her in the little back room that she and Giles used as a study, hunched over the bright screen of the laptop. She spun round with a gasp when she sensed I was there.

'Sorry, I didn't mean to make you jump,' I said.

'No! No, I was finishing off some work,' she said.

'You shouldn't hunch over the screen like that, it's bad for your back.'

'Yeah, well . . . ' She shrugged and I watched as she shut everything down with quick, tense movements. I could see I'd interrupted something.

'I didn't mean to stop you. You carry on . . . '

'No, like I said, just boring old work. It's nothing.'

'Becky?'

She looked up again and I saw that she was tired. I wondered if she'd been up late last night with all this work.

'Yes?'

'We don't want to sponge off you. And . . . you know my father sold Pops's house? Well, there must be some way of getting the money out. The money belongs to Pops, so . . . '

'Dom, listen. The bottom line is, we can't risk you being

traced, and any move you make to try and get a job or access an account would be traceable immediately. We're your friends, for goodness' sake. We can feed you for a while yet, OK?'

She was cross with me. Offended, perhaps, because I couldn't accept their generosity without going on about it. Or perhaps she was just tired. Either way, now wasn't the right time to ask about using the computer. And then Giles appeared, saying that a woodworm man was here and wanted to look in the loft.

'Apparently the roof's a bit saggy and it might be to do with the timbers,' he said.

'Oh, no! Will that cost a fortune?' said Becky.

'Don't know. Want to come and look?'

They went off to investigate. I looked at the laptop. It occurred to me that I'd need to check if Becky had the right programmes for dealing with artwork. If not, the whole project would have to wait until I could buy software. It wouldn't take a minute just to have a quick look.

I switched the thing on, meaning to just check through the icons on the screen, but then the email icon started to flash. My hand moved to the mouse. I knew that I shouldn't do this, but something made me—curiosity about Becky's work, perhaps. Anyhow, I did it. I clicked on the icon. The message that flashed up nearly stopped my heartbeat.

Becky, I know who Dominic Gordon is. You were always a good journalist and you know it's in the public interest for this story to be told. I'd like to have you on board, get your angle. Call me.

My face burned and my heart hammered as if I'd been caught stealing. With my hand shaking so badly I could hardly control the mouse, I scrolled up and down to see if there was any more but there wasn't. Then I went to the sender's address. It was from someone calling themselves

197

Trackerdog. And there was an attachment. I opened it and saw a picture of a beach resort. I had a memory of that scene. I struggled to think where from. A holiday? And then the memory surged back, with a panic that gripped my throat. It was a scan of the postcard that Mum had sent to Giles from the Cayman Islands. I scrolled down and there, underneath the picture, was the back of the card with her handwriting.

'. . . *As you can see, we are now in the Cayman Islands at the generous invitation of Professor Holt, who is here doing some research and kindly felt that the break might do us good. In a way it is of some comfort to be close to someone who knew Nick so well* . . . '

As I scrolled I saw something else beneath it. Trackerdog had gone to the trouble of magnifying the postmark area, just in case Becky missed the point. The stamp and mark clearly identified the postcard as being from the Cayman Islands. It was posted on 30 March 2001. And then there was the last thing, the thing that sent a cold bolt of shock through me. A copy of my birth certificate. A boy. Born to Michael and Carla Gordon. 1st January 2002.

I slumped back in the chair. Rain tapped and trickled at the window and the grey sky dulled the tiny room so that the only patch of brightness came from the laptop screen. The cursor was pulsating, taunting.

I lurched forwards, grabbed the mouse and clicked Reply. I typed fast in huge letters, *Get away from me and stay away! Leave me alone. You don't know who I am. You don't understand what you're doing. If you come after me, I'll* . . .

I'll what? How I hated people who made me feel helpless! I typed the words: *KILL YOU*. Then I whizzed the cursor up to Send. Becky's scream from the doorway stopped me.

'NO! For God's sake, don't!'

198

I spun round. Becky came into the room, with Giles just behind her.

'Is it Trackerdog again?' she asked.

'The postcard,' I said in a wobbly voice. 'Look . . . '

I watched Becky as she read the message and the attachment. She could betray me if she wanted. It would be easy. One word from her and I'd be all over the media. In the public interest. She looked up at Giles, her eyes huge and dark in her pale face.

'She's been through your rooms at Grenville Hall!' she said.

Giles was distraught. 'I never thought of the damned postcard! I *should* have!'

'Tell me what's happening!' I managed to say. But I already knew who 'she' was.

Giles slumped onto the sofa with a sigh. 'We're pretty certain it's Leanne Kelsey.'

'It was just about the unluckiest thing that could have happened, you two bumping into her in Cambridge that day,' said Becky. 'Because she knew Nick so well—she used to go out with him.'

'How long has she been doing this?' I whispered, fear squeezing at my voice. It probably *had* been her at the monorail station, then. She was tracking me.

'About a week. She's been sending messages. She seems to have made the assumption that you'll either be with your parents or with us. I suspect she's sending this stuff to your father as well. Anyway, there's a mask on this email address, so she can't trace us . . . '

'A week? And you didn't tell me!'

'We didn't want to worry you,' said Becky.

'Oh, don't give me that! When I'm hunted down like a rat in a hole, how worried d'you think I'm going to be then?'

'Dominic, don't . . . ' she began.

'NO!' I cried, panic raging through me now. 'I need to know what's happening! I'm sick of being helpless! I'm sick of people trying to control every bit of my life! You've got no right to treat me like a kid! You're not my bloody mother!'

She leapt up and out of the room. Giles shot me an icy look and strode over to the laptop. He switched it off and walked out with it, slamming the door behind him.

I stood in the darkening room, shaking with anger. At them, at that Kelsey bitch, at everyone. They hadn't trusted me to cope with the truth, nobody ever had. And now it was all over. Leanne Kelsey had probably already sold the story.

I bashed out of the room, grabbed my coat and headed out of the cottage and up into the pinewoods.

38

With pain searing through my lungs, I charged up through the woods, alongside the swollen river and on up into the mountains. Pretty soon I was soaked through, my feet squelching in my boots as they sent stones flying with every angry step.

There was a terror chasing me, but I couldn't escape it because it was coming from inside. It was the dream I'd had at home. The fish nibbling pieces out of me. I'd be entertainment for the crowds. The only human clone in the world. Got to get his story, test him, examine him, splash him all over the media. Everyone would want a piece of the property, they'd all have an opinion. Not natural, a freak. Journalists and TV presenters would pick over my life, gouging out juicy bits and, if they couldn't find what they wanted, they'd make it up. That's what celebrities say they do, anyway, and I used to think, well, that's what they should expect, if they want to be famous. But I didn't want to be famous. Not for this.

In no time at all I was higher than I'd been before, heading up towards huge dark buttresses of rock that shored up the biggest of the mountains, the one directly overlooking the lake. There was a sort of path and I struggled on up it, up the steeply rising ground with its sharp, slithering scree. Dangerous territory, especially in the wet. So what? Perhaps it would be the best thing if I were found, smashed and mangled, at the bottom of the mountain. Solve everyone's problems. Then I had this absurd vision of my father scraping up the remains and having me re-cloned. That made me laugh and I laughed so much that I cried and soon I didn't know whether the wetness coursing down my face was from tears or the lashing rain.

I was climbing now, using my hands as well as my legs to claw my way upwards. I'd lost the path. I seemed to be heading towards the ridge that linked this mountain with the next. I stopped, struggling to gulp enough air, my head swimming, and looked up. There was a sheer cliff dead ahead of me, plunging down to a near-vertical scree slope and from there into the black water of the lake below. I saw that if I could get round the cliff and get myself above it, I might be able to make it onto the ridge. I changed course, working my way across the slope below the cliff. But even as I worked my way round, the gradient got steeper and steeper until I couldn't stand up at all but had to try and clamp onto the mountainside, keeping my centre of gravity as close to it as I could. If I fell backwards I would be straight into that bottomless black water. Once, I looked down, imagining the lake as deep as the mountain was high. I didn't look down again.

Once I was round the cliff, the only way was up and it was steep. I began grabbing at the coarse, sharp-bladed grass, at earth, at rocks that gave way the moment I trusted my weight to them. Suddenly, a rock came clean away under my hand and crashed down to the water below. I began to slide down after it. I gouged the toes of my boots into the scree, clinging on for my life, and, after long moments, I managed to stop the slide. But I knew that any second I could start again, sliding faster and faster and then falling backwards. A cold sweat of absolute terror drenched over me and my arms and legs began to shake uncontrollably, all the strength gone from them. I knew that if I couldn't calm my mind and my body and keep on going up, I was dead meat. I clung to the mountain for long moments, eyes closed against the rain, until my heartbeat calmed. Then I opened my eyes, looked up and chose a rock just above my head that I could reach and that looked as if it would take my weight. I stretched out a hand, grabbed the rock, and hauled myself up. The rock gave way just as I managed to grab another and then another, pushing and pulling myself on and up, faster and faster as the land slid beneath me, until at last I saw that, instead of more rock above me, there was sky. Sky grey with mizzly cloud. I'd made it to the ridge.

I scrambled the last metre and landed on my belly. I could see that the ridge was very narrow, with an outcrop of rocks in one direction, the summit of the mountain. In the other direction was a broad slab from which there was what looked like a path down.

I staggered on all fours along the ridge to the summit and wedged myself into a hollow in the rocks. I sat there until my heartbeat slowed to normal, and then I don't know how long after that.

I sat there trying to think of anything, anything I could do to stop the media show getting me. Perhaps Imogen and my father had been right. I could have been in Australia now, with a new identity. I tried to imagine what that would be like. Perhaps it still wasn't too late.

My thoughts plunged and crashed like waves, time passed and all my anger ebbed away. A great, empty loneliness washed over me. As if I was the last person on the planet, huddled into rock, unable to move.

The afternoon light was fading. Above the ridges and peaks around me, the sky was bruised purple and yellow and pink. I knew I couldn't sit on the mountain for ever. Slowly, I eased my stiff limbs out of the hollow of rock and stood up. I picked my way along the ridge and found a path.

As I came down onto the lower slopes I heard voices

calling for me and then saw Giles and Becky stumbling over the slippery rocks by the river, their waterproof coats glistening and dripping.

Giles saw me first and stood blinking through the rain, his arms flailing as he tried to keep balance. 'Where the bloody hell have you been?' he yelled.

'Up the mountain,' I said.

'Good view?'

Becky swiped at him. 'Shut up, Giles!' She swept the trickling strings of hair from her face and gave me a weak smile.

'We've been trying to imagine how you feel, and of course we can't,' she said. 'I'm sorry, Dom. I shouldn't try and protect you—I couldn't, anyway. Will you come home and see what I've been working on?'

'I'm sorry too, really sorry about what I said. I just felt . . . trapped.'

'We know,' said Giles. 'Come on, you'd better have the first bath.'

Later, when Pops was fast asleep and I was wrapped in Giles's bath robe by the fire in the little back room, Becky set up the laptop to show me what she'd been doing. I watched as the screen burst into light. She clicked on a folder with a list of print and TV media titles and dates.

'I've kept track of everything that Leanne has written in the print news, and I think I've got all the TV and Net stuff too,' she said. 'You can read through them at your leisure, of course, but I'll just show you one that sets the tone. This is her angle on cloning.'

She selected a file and I read.

'The aim of cloning is to make one person as an exact copy of another who is already living or has lived and died. Freaky, isn't it? It means that the rich and famous don't need to die. They can live on . . . and on and on. And in a world where status is everything, eternal existence is the

204

ultimate status symbol—let's face it, can you think of a better one? Or take the case of rich parents who have the misfortune to lose a child. Wishart or others like him could replace that child. There is no death for those who can afford to break man's law—and God's law. Wishart knew there was a hell of a lot of money to be made from this.

'And if Wishart, an obscure doctor with an unremarkable academic record, can have a go at cloning an "entire" human, then what, we may ask, have our more eminent scientists been up to since the arrival of that first momentous sheep? Have any of them succeeded where Wishart failed? Some burning questions remain unanswered. Like—who taught Wishart this sophisticated medical technique? And how many cute little freaks of nature might we have running around, unnoticed, in our midst?'

'This is rubbish!' I said. 'Why doesn't she write about it properly?'

'Because she's in the business of selling sensational stories,' said Becky.

'But she should tell the truth!'

'Who knows what the truth is?' said Becky. 'All the while you can play on misconceptions and prejudices and invent a good yarn, you're selling the story. She could make a fortune out of you. You're the greatest news scoop of the twenty-first century. Probably of any century—because you're unique.'

'Because I'm *not* unique,' I said.

'Smart-arse,' said Giles. 'The point is, Becky's been watching really carefully and she reckons Leanne is the only one who knows—or thinks she knows—about you. Nobody else has gone anywhere near Imogen. We're pretty sure Leanne will keep this to herself until she's certain of her ground.'

'But she *is* certain, isn't she?' I said. 'The email linking the postcard and my birth certificate . . .'

'It's still not conclusive proof,' said Giles. 'There's absolutely no reason why your mother shouldn't have conceived naturally during that holiday. Leanne would need solid evidence from Wishart or some other witness as to what Imogen was doing, or a confession from Imogen herself. Remember, she'd be incriminating the woman who made paralysed people walk again. She'd have to be *so* certain of her facts . . .'

'There is one other way she could get proof,' said Becky, 'and that's by cross-matching your DNA with Nick's. They'd be identical, of course, and that would prove that biologically you are twins.'

'Twins. Yes, I've thought about that.' I remembered the twins at the Link.

'Identical twins,' said Becky, 'born twenty-two years apart. It's a really long shot, but if there was any way of carbon-dating a sample to show that Dominic's DNA existed before he himself was born . . .'

'I don't think we need worry about that,' said Giles. 'No one would have a sample of Nick's tissue. Not now, it was so long ago.'

'Imogen might,' I said, 'but I think she destroyed everything she had.'

'It wouldn't take much,' said Becky, 'a single hair would do it.'

'You mean, they'd be carbon-dating a sample to show that it *couldn't* be Dominic's—because he wasn't alive then—even though it had identical DNA?' said Giles. 'That really is a long-shot. Can carbon-dating be that accurate?'

'I don't know,' sighed Becky.

I clicked back to the postcard and, with a pang, looked at Mum's extravagant, flowing handwriting. 'You know, I think she knows she can't get proof,' I said. 'Otherwise what's this emailing stuff about? She's trying to frighten us into reacting. Or else, I suppose . . .'

'What?' said Becky.

'Or else tempt you into handing me over.'

'Well, you can put that idea right out of your head, and so can she!' said Giles.

'I know, I'm sorry, I never really thought you would.'

'What do you want to do?' he asked softly.

The answer came without me even thinking about it. 'I want to get on with things,' I said, 'with my painting, for however much time I have left before they find me.'

'It's not certain they *will* find you, you know.'

'Nothing's certain, is it?' I said.

There was a silence, and then Becky said, 'I want to keep watching, if that's all right with you. She may well try and get to Wishart in prison . . .'

'Does she know there's a link between Wishart and Imogen?' I said.

'She's obviously working on the hunch that Wishart learned the technique from Imogen, so if she can get him to talk she'll discover that he was actually there when . . . when you were conceived,' said Becky.

'And why wouldn't Wishart talk?' I said. 'He's got nothing to lose.'

I shut the laptop down and we sat in a circle of pale light from the overhead bulb. Outside, the wind rustled the lakeside rowan trees and it sounded for all the world like the whispering of a gathering crowd.

39

It was a couple of days after this that I woke in the morning to the sound of tapping at my door. It creaked open and there was Becky. She held out a letter.

'It came in a separate envelope addressed to me at Cambridge. Our neighbour forwarded it.'

I recognized Mum's handwriting at once and tore it open. I rubbed my bleary eyes and read.

Darling, Margi told me that you're with Giles and Becky. I pray that it's true. I know they're not at home because your father has been trying to find them.

I'm in a drying-out clinic. I don't want you to worry about this—it means I'm determined to get better and be a proper mother. I don't know what your father intends to do. He knows you have Pops with you but he has no idea where you are. Can you let me know if you are with Giles and Becky? You can call the number below. If you call on an hour—any hour—and let it ring four times and then hang up, I'll know it's you and I won't worry any more. I'm longing to hear your voice but I won't answer because I think he's had my phone bugged. God, I hope you're with them. You can trust Giles with your life.

Love you, love you, love you
   Mum

'What's the time?' I asked Becky.
'Five to eight.'
'Right, I've got to phone her in five minutes.'
'Dom, be careful, your father might have bugged the . . . '

I grinned. 'He has. Mum's got a code for us to use. And don't worry, I'll dial up and put a screen on our number.'

'You're getting good at being a fugitive, aren't you?'

She smiled and reached down for the torn envelope I'd discarded. 'Hey, have you seen inside this? She's sent you some money.'

I looked. Typical Mum, she'd gone over the top and sent loads of cash. Not that I was complaining. I bounced myself back onto the bed.

'Great! Now I can help with the tuna and doughnut bills,' I said. 'It's about time!'

I rang the number dead on eight o'clock and let it ring four times, imagining her waiting, imagining her smile when there was no fifth ring. And then I threw on some clothes, threw down some breakfast, and borrowed Becky's bike to go into the village. I could tell Giles and Becky didn't really want me to go, but they didn't try to stop me. I pedalled like mad and then freewheeled down the hills, loving the rush of breeze against me.

We were going to be all right. I was going to put my family back together again. Mum would stop drinking, we'd find a nice place to live up here and I could get on with my artwork, maybe even go to college. We'd look after Pops and keep him supplied with chocolate doughnuts for ever.

I stopped in the main street of the little village, where there was a likely-looking stationer's shop, and leaned the bike with some others against the stone wall opposite. I wandered into the shop and saw that it doubled as a newsagent's. It was no surprise to find that the two remaining copies of national newspapers had Wishart's face staring out of them. 'Should this man die?' ran the headline. We'd been watching the news and there'd been a whole lot of stuff about whether they should execute

Wishart after all. If they went ahead and did it, I was out of danger, assuming that no one had already made a connection between him and Imogen. Dead men don't talk, as Giles had said. Did this mean that I wanted Wishart dead? I didn't want to think about that. Because the nightmare that kept flooding into my mind was about Imogen. If they found out what Imogen had done they'd certainly kill her. They did it by lethal injection. Strapped you to a bed and put you down like a dog. They'd been through it all on TV in gory detail. Which drugs are used, what the person would feel. How long it takes.

Keep yourself safe, Imogen, I spoke to her in my mind. For God's sake, keep yourself safe and I'll keep myself safe and we'll all be fine.

I stared at the familiar face of Wishart, the bald head, the tiny eyes with the smug smile. Then, feeling as if I was being stared at myself, I looked up and saw a bunch of people at the far end of the shop. They were all looking my way.

'Sorry, laddie, there's not much to choose from,' said the woman behind the counter. 'Someone's just come in wanting one of each and it's cleaned us out of most of the national papers.'

'Oh, that's OK,' I said, 'I was after some drawing pads if you have them.'

'Down the far end,' smiled the woman. 'There's pencils, brushes, and a small selection of paints down there too.'

They turned back to their conversation and one of them, a young woman who was rocking a babycart backwards and forwards, said, 'It's against nature!'

Carefully, I glanced at the group again.

'Undoubtedly,' said an old man, 'but supposing you had a poor wee child that died and you could bring her back, would you do it, if you could?'

'Ah, now. If you really thought you could do *that*,'

said the woman behind the counter, 'that it was possible to bring a child back from the dead, how could you *not* do it?'

'Yes, but that's not what this couple were trying to do,' said the mother. 'They only wanted a baby that looked a certain way. What would have happened if something had gone wrong and it had been born ugly? Would they have loved it just the same?'

'Hmmm.' The woman behind the counter came out with a pile of magazines and thumped them down near me. 'Whatever they say, it's my belief that nature always finds a way of fighting back. They can fiddle around all they like, but nature is cleverer than all of us.'

'It's wickedness in the sight of the Lord!' said a surly-looking woman. She banged her basket down on the counter. 'Frankenstein all over again—and look what happened there!'

'Frankenstein is only a story, Mrs McAuliffe,' said the old man.

'Hmmph!' said Mrs McAuliffe.

That seemed to finish the subject and I went up to the counter to pay for the pads, paints, and coloured pencils I'd chosen.

'Budding artist?' asked the shopkeeper.

'Trying to be.' I smiled.

She had a kind face and I liked what she'd said about nature being cleverer than any of us, but what would she say to me—what would any of them say—if they knew what I was?

I stepped out into the bright morning and went to retrieve Becky's bike, noticing as I did so that the expensive-looking ladies' mountain bike that someone had kindly leant on top of it probably belonged to the person who had cleaned the shop out of papers. Wishart's face, again, was staring at me from a saddle-bag stuffed to

211

bursting. I carefully moved the bike to get at Becky's, then mounted up and pedalled for home as hard as I could.

As I came down the drive I saw Becky down by the lake. I propped the bike up and was about to call out to her when Giles came lolloping out of the cottage with a champagne bottle in one hand and a fistful of glasses in the other. He gestured to me and I gathered that I was to keep quiet because he was going to creep up on Becky and surprise her. The trouble was, he had nothing on his feet and as we'd recently cut the long, rough grass of the lawn it wasn't exactly a barefoot surface. He picked his way through the prickly stubble with stifled shrieks and curses, dropped the glasses, and finally fell over. Becky swung round, laughing.

'Surprise, surprise!' I yelled.

I reached them just as Giles had got to his feet and discovered that the glasses weren't broken.

'What's the celebration?' I asked.

'All signed, sealed, and delivered,' said Giles. 'This dilapidated cottage with the horribly dangerous lawn is officially ours as from today!'

We cracked open the champagne and Pops took charge—not very successfully—of cooking a sausage lunch on the camp fire.

I caught myself watching Becky and Giles as they spread out a blanket and got together the plates, forks, and tongs for Pops. The way they laughed with and at each other, the way they touched each other, listened to each other. Becky caught me watching.

'What're you thinking?' she asked, licking her fingers and leaning back against Giles.

'I was thinking about . . . I suppose I was thinking about the things I think.'

'Lost me there,' said Giles. 'Or at least, I think you have.'

'What I mean is,' I grinned, 'I mean—everything that Nick saw and thought and felt when he was alive made him what he was, and everything that I see and feel and think has made me . . . *is* making me, because it changes every day. It isn't copyable, all that, is it, even if your genes can be copied?'

'You mean, cloning is only gene deep?' laughed Becky.

'Yes! That's exactly what I mean!'

I looked out across the bright surface of the lake. I was beginning to feel OK with all of that. I was working it out and it would be OK. I knew now that the real problem wasn't to do with *how* I got here, it was to do with *why*. I'd been ordered for a purpose. That's what the woman with the babycart had meant. What happens if things go wrong and the parents don't get the baby they ordered?

'A new kind of orphan,' I murmured.

'What?' said Becky, squinting at me.

At that moment we were all distracted by something rustling under the shoreline trees around the little bay. A couple of ducks shot out from the shadows, flapping their wings crossly before re-folding them and gliding away.

'Grebes,' said Pops. 'Or perhaps not.'

And because there was champagne and we were all so happy, and because Pops decided he wanted a haircut and I made a hash of it because of the champagne, and because all four of us ended up giggling helplessly, none of us noticed the person in the rowing boat beneath the shoreline trees. But I know now that they must have been there, watching.

40

The day scheduled for Wishart's execution was the first time I noticed the rowing boat on the lake. There was someone fishing from it. I glanced down now and then from my vantage point high up in the outcrop of rocks at the end of the ridge. I'd climbed up here often, after that first time. Now it felt like my 'safe' place, where I could just switch off and concentrate on my work. I was here to do my final sketches from this viewpoint and tomorrow I would begin a new piece of work, the last in my series for the set of cards.

But I couldn't concentrate properly that day. My mind wasn't gelling with the mountains. I kept thinking of the man I'd never met, waiting in a cell, counting out the last hours of his life. At least it looked as though Imogen was safe. She'd made no more appearances on TV and there'd been no interviews asking her opinion about the Wishart case.

All sorts of things had come out about what Wishart had promised his customers, how he could guarantee that their baby would be just as they wanted it. He'd started with the gene-screens, selecting the right eye colour, the right IQ, or saying he could guarantee that the 'outcome' would be a fast runner or good at music. And then he'd gone for the big one—an 'entire' cloned baby. You can have yourself copied, he'd boasted in one recorded phone conversation. No one would ever know—after all, how many kids bear an uncanny resemblance to one or other of their parents?

I fidgeted against the cold rock at my back and glanced

down at the lake again. The boat was still there, but it had drifted further towards our little bay.

I began to work in charcoal, an angry sketch of the cruel gashes on the mountain face opposite. I couldn't bear to think of anyone taking that lethal injection into their arm, but I hated Wishart. Offering to make kids to order as if they were fashion accessories. The sketch began to take shape as I focused my energy and let myself see the shapes carved out by millennia of eruption, water, and wind.

Later, as it began to get cold, I packed up and, balancing my rucksack carefully, began to pick my way back across the ridge. The rowing boat was long gone and the shadows of clouds were darkening the lake. I was halfway across when a distant drumming at the still mountain air stopped me. I listened hard as the sound shaped itself into the thudding of a helicopter. Way in the distance at first, but then growing louder, echoing off the rock. I couldn't tell which direction it was coming from. I spun round, nearly losing my footing, and swayed, with the sheer drop below me, before scrambling across to the safety of the granite slab beyond. I stood up. Still there was no way of telling where the thing was coming from. My heart began to race.

Suddenly the shadow shot out onto the lake from the narrow valley at its head and seconds later the sound was hammering off the rock walls of our valley as the machine itself skimmed fast and low over the water. I began to run as best I could over the rocky ground, leaping and stumbling. I hadn't seen the markings on the helicopter, so I couldn't be certain it was my father's, but I *felt* it was. I knew I had to get to the cottage before he did.

It was hopeless. As I ran down towards the river I saw the water of our lake being whipped into furious circles and the upper branches of the lakeside rowan trees flailing in the wind as the helicopter prepared to land on our lawn.

I leaped from boulder to boulder beside the river and

raced down through the dark pinewoods. Giles wasn't at home, but I knew my father would have a go at Becky, and he'd upset Pops. I stopped, gasping for breath at the edge of the woods, because another thought had come. What if it wasn't him? What if it was someone else? Maybe we'd been tracked. If Leanne Kelsey or anyone else really *had* made the connection between Wishart, Imogen, and me, how hard would it be to find me? I hesitated at the edge of the back lawn, watching the cottage. And then I saw a tall, broad body move across the kitchen window. I heard bursts of the familiar bullying shout.

I ran across the lawn and barged through the kitchen door. There he was, in his expensive clothes, the sickly musk of his aftershave filling the tiny kitchen. Becky was leaning against the sink, arms folded, face drawn.

'Well, here we are, then,' said my father, showing no sign of surprise. He allowed himself a sarcastic grin. 'Rebecca here was foolishly attempting to convince me that you had moved on—who knows when to who knows where? Get your things together, we haven't much time.'

I felt the force of him, waiting, expecting to be obeyed. I met the icy blue eyes.

We stared at each other. I saw that nothing had changed. It had made no difference that I'd run away. He didn't care what I felt. He still thought he was invincible.

'NOW, Dominic,' he said.

'I'm not going anywhere,' I said. My heart was hammering so hard I was sure he could see it, but I knew I had to keep going. I had to win.

'Dominic, I don't think you comprehend the seriousness of the situation you're in. Had you not embarked upon your course of interfering, things might have been—'

'INTERFERING?' I yelled. The word had burst out in anger, but now I'd started I kept going. 'I try to find out about my brother and uncover all your lies and your *criminal* secrets and you call it interfering! *You* interfered! You're the one that interfered with Nick, with *me*, with *Mum*. With all our lives! Haven't you anything to say about that? Haven't you anything . . . '

My voice shook out of control. I couldn't find the words any more.

Becky reached out to touch my arm. My father looked at us, and then a horrible sneer spread across his face. 'Oh, very cosy,' he said, 'though isn't he rather young for you, Rebecca? Does Giles know about this?'

I don't know where the force came from but it came hard and fast and with such rage that my father had reeled backwards and was clutching at his jaw before I even felt the pain in my fist.

'Dominic!' screamed Becky.

I watched him recover his balance and wipe a hand across his mouth. For a split second I saw him looking shocked. Not from the pain but because I'd dared to hit him. But it didn't last long. He turned to face me, as calm as ever.

'Dominic, the point I'm trying to get across to you is that you are in danger. It really would be wise to listen carefully to what I'm going to say.'

My heart was crashing at my ribs. My fist hurt. I took a deep breath and said, 'All right. Go on.'

'The execution has taken place,' he said. 'Wishart is dead. I'm not surprised. There's little point in having a death penalty if it's not going to be enforced. My guess is that they needed to make an example of him. In any case he was, by all accounts, a rather unpleasant little man.'

'Does that make a difference?' said Becky.

He settled his patronizing gaze on her.

'Rebecca, what you have clearly failed to learn is that mankind is made up of the great people and the little people. Wishart was undoubtedly one of the little people,

217

otherwise he wouldn't have been so stupid as to have been caught. However, we can't discount the possibility that he may have talked before he was executed. And if he talked, Dominic, you have only one chance of escaping media attention. So you *will* come to Australia with us.'

'Yes,' I said, 'I'd like to go to Australia.'

He flapped his coat closed and gestured towards the door.

'I'd like to paint the landscape and the animals,' I said. 'I might do that in my gap year, if I decide to go to art college. I might work my way round Australia. But whatever I do, *I'll* choose. And now I choose to stay here and I'm not going anywhere with you.'

'Choice is one thing you don't have, you stupid little boy!' roared my father. 'If the media get hold of you they'll crucify you! It only takes one journalist to get the right story or even *think* they've got the right story!'

'And they'll crucify you too. Is that what you're worried about? That's why you want to go to Australia. I won't come with you! Why should I? You've never loved me and I don't love you!'

I felt Becky tense up behind me as my father came towards us. His face, so clean and smooth, so good looking, was twisting into an ugly rage.

'I'm not Nick, Dad. You've *got* to understand it. I am not the same person. You can clone a body but you can't clone a brain. Ask Imogen if you don't believe me. I've got my own life, my own things I want to do. *Please understand*, Dad.'

And that did what the punch couldn't do. It made him look, really look, at me. And as we stood staring at each other in the silence of the kitchen, I sensed that he couldn't understand what he was seeing. I looked so much like Nick. Exactly the same fifteen-year-old face that he'd had. Probably even the same voice. A slight frown flicked over my father's brow and something was happening to his eyes. It was almost as if the blue was fading. Something inside him was dying, a cloud sweeping over the mountain, and I understood that in order to talk honestly, to really share respect and understanding, he'd have to give up some of his power. The one thing that gave him a sense of who he was. Suddenly, I felt sorry.

'Look, Dad,' I said, 'I've really started to work on my painting. There's one here that I've done of the mountains, look. Please look at it, Dad, *please*.' I pointed to the painting that was propped up to dry on the table behind him. He didn't turn. His eyes wandered to Becky. She moved forward as if to touch his arm.

'Mr Gordon, I know how much you loved him . . . '

He swiped his arm upwards and I thought he was going to hit her, but he didn't. He spun round and left the cottage. A few minutes later we heard the helicopter take off.

41

The days began to shorten and the colours of our landscape changed.

Each morning, on those first days following the execution, I would go to the laptop. Trackerdog had gone quiet, so I began to believe that I'd been right. Leanne couldn't prove her case. She hadn't got anything out of Wishart, even if she'd been allowed to see him. I also checked all the news items on the laptop to watch what the rest of the media were doing. Like a pack of jackals, they were devouring the last few scraps of the meal.

First they went after the couple for whom Wishart had tried to clone the baby. There was a live news item from the States announcing that the ex-model, her husband, and their three boys had attempted to hide. But they'd been found. The pictures showed the woman trying to get to a waiting car, her three boys struggling to follow her through a jeering crush of people. The older boy was trying to protect his brothers, the youngest of whom was only a little kid, about six, I reckoned. Someone grabbed the little boy, pulling his T-shirt so hard that it spun him round. A voice yelled, 'Are you a clone too, kid?' The little boy began to cry and at last his mother turned back to help him. The newscaster added that speculation that the youngest boy was a clone of the father had been rigorously denied but the couple had refused to subject the child to the DNA testing that would prove it.

After a few days of hounding the couple, the media seemed to lose interest and my searches came up with only a few pieces from women's magazines and then a letter in a leading newspaper from some eighty-year-old nutcase in Cornwall who reckoned he was a clone. 'And have been all my life,' he wrote.

During this time, I was trying to finish the last painting for my set of cards, but it wouldn't come right. I wanted to paint the changing colours around me, the goldening of the greens and the colder, deeper shadows in the mountains. But it wouldn't come, and after days of trying, I'd had enough.

So, one morning I put away my art things and went to see what I could do to make myself useful. Chopping logs seemed favourite. Pops wanted to help by stacking everything I chopped into the lean-to woodshed and he tottered back and forth, back and forth with armfuls, his breath clouding out on the damp air. I was getting worried.

'Pops, you shouldn't be doing this. I can stack them. You go and rest.'

He didn't answer, didn't even seem to hear me.

'Pops, are you all right? Pops!'

He turned, dropped the armful he was carrying, and hung his head.

'Didn't know how to put things right,' he said. 'Didn't know what to do.'

He began shaking his hand by his side, his own personal distress signal. I felt my own heartbeat quicken as I asked, 'What things, Pops? Put what things right?'

'I should have helped her.'

'You mean Mum?'

His watery old eyes wandered round my face and he nodded.

'Come and sit down, Pops.' I led him to the sagging bench that leaned against the wall of the cottage. I could hardly breathe, my heart was pounding so much. I waited for it to calm, but it didn't. 'Pops . . . you've known all along, haven't you? About me . . . me and Nick? You hid the photo album when you knew I'd found it, didn't you?'

He turned and grabbed my arm with surprising force.

'The bastard, in his helicopter! Don't let him break you, Dominic. Not like he did your mother.'

'What do you mean, Pops? How did he break her?'

'Wouldn't let her go. She wanted to bring you home, when you were a baby.'

'She wanted to bring me back to England? You mean, she wanted to leave Dad?'

He nodded again. 'When you were a baby. I should have helped her!'

I stared down at the first of the fallen leaves: honey, yellow, and red. So she had tried to make a stand. But of course he'd never have let her go, taking with her his second chance with Nick. Taking such a huge secret.

'Pops, whatever happened then, it couldn't have been your fault!' I said. 'You mustn't ever think that! And you did help! When we did come back to England, you helped *me*! You let me do my painting at your house. I had nowhere else to go. I'd have got nowhere without you!'

'Crushed the spirit out of her,' he whispered.

'Pops, listen! He *didn't* crush the spirit out of her. She's getting better. And we're going to get a new house together, the three of us. Up here in Scotland.'

'We are?'

'Yes.'

I'd surprised myself, saying out loud what I wanted to happen. I saw disbelief, hope, relief, and joy wash over his tired old face and I knew then that I had to *make* it happen. It was the final thing that had to be fixed and then we'd be all right again.

'You go in now, Pops,' I said, rubbing my hand over

222

his and feeling the coldness of it. 'It's nearly lunchtime anyhow. I'll finish stacking the logs.'

He eased himself up from the bench and stood for a few seconds. Then he leaned back down, brought his cold, shaking hand to my cheek and kissed me on the head.

'Good fellow!' He patted my cheek gently. 'See about lunch.'

He wandered inside and I sat a few moments more, wondering how to get hold of Mum. Then I jumped up. There were loads of things I could try. Phoning the number she gave me and letting it ring. She might answer now that Dad had found out where I was anyway. Or I could try Margi, perhaps? Even my dad's number. He'd have to know where she was, wouldn't he?

I got the logs stacked in no time and took some in for the evening's fire. Then I dialled the number for Mum's drying-out clinic and let it ring and ring. Eventually I got through to a switchboard operator who told me Mum had left but she wouldn't tell me where she'd gone. 'Company policy,' she said primly. 'Patient confidentiality.'

So I tried Mum's mobile, which was as dead as a dodo. First thing we'd have to do in our new lives was to get Mum to bond with her mobile, even if I had to chain it to her wrist, I thought as I dialled Margi's number.

'Margaret Thompson speaking. Hello?'

'Margi!' I cried. 'It's me! Dominic!'

'Dominic! Sweetheart! Oh goodness, what a coincidence! Are you safe?' Her voice bounced down the line. I could hear something else in the background, too.

'Yes, I'm safe. Why a coincidence?'

'Sweetheart, I've got your mum here with me.'

I'd half-known it already. I'd recognized the squeals in the background. I was handed over.

'Darling!' cried Mum. 'Are you safe? How's Pops?'

I slid my back down the bumpy whitewashed wall of

the hallway and sat on the stone floor, tears close at the sound of her voice.

'We're both fine. Giles and Becky have been great. The cottage is great, and the mountains . . . But, Mum . . . Dad's been and we've had one heck of a row. I'm really sorry.'

'Don't be, Dominic,' she said. 'It isn't your fault. If your father wants a relationship with either of us now, he's got to take some steps towards us. And I have to say he's got some distance to cover, literally and metaphorically. He's gone to Australia.'

'Right.' I was trying to take it all in. Not just the news of my father's departure from these shores. I'd half expected that. Not just my own desperate relief at hearing her. The real thing, the real change, was in Mum. I could feel it through her voice. The anxiety had gone, the expectation of hurt or defeat that had always rung through the music of her voice, had changed to something else. Not something brash or bullying, like some of these celebrity types who bang on about how they've learnt to assert themselves. This was a different note. A note of calm.

'I've been sorting out some money,' she said. 'We need to decide where we want to base ourselves, what we're going to do. And Pops is all right? That's wonderful.'

'Yes, he is, but . . .'

'Yes . . . ?'

'But he needs you. We both need you.'

'You've got me. And I mean all of me from now on.'

My throat hurt with a sudden, swelling tension. I understood. She'd cracked it, then, the drinking. We were on our way to being a proper family for the first time.

'Darling, there's something else you should know,' she said. 'Imogen's been in touch. She wanted to know where you were. I told her you were safe in Scotland with Giles and Becky.'

'What? Oh, Mum, that's how Dad found me! She'd have gone straight to him, like last time!'

'No, it was *after* your father found you. I told Imogen because she was so worried about you. She said it was important, she needed to know where you were. I said I didn't know exactly but that your father did. She may have called him, I don't know. In any case, they can't harm us now. The story's over.'

'It'd better be,' I said.

I glanced down the hallway and saw Pops moving back and forth across the kitchen doorway with pans and plates.

'Do you want to speak to Pops?' I asked.

'Yes. Just give me your number first and as soon as I've got everything in place I'll be up to see you all. Should be a couple of days.'

'Really? That's great!'

I gave her the number and then went to get Pops. I left him to talk to her, his face wide with smile as he picked up the receiver. I wandered outside and found Giles up a ladder putting the finishing touches to the paintwork on the eaves.

'Mum's coming,' I said.

'Really? That's good, Dom, I'm so glad!' He grinned down at me.

'She's getting things sorted out with money. I'm wondering if we could buy a place up here.'

'There are worse places to live,' he said. 'I suppose you ought to do a recce around the schools and colleges, see what they have to offer before you decide.'

'Hmm,' I said. 'I'd like to go to art college one day, if I can get in.'

'Course you'll get in!' He clambered down the ladder and fiddled about wiping the brush and closing up the paint tin. 'You're certainly better at painting than I am!'

He beamed at me and I saw that there was more white paint on him—in his hair, on his clothes, and on his hands—than there was on the cottage.

'Seriously, though,' he said, 'if you find what you're good at and work to get better at it—then that's all any of us can do, isn't it?'

'Yeah.' I grinned.

At that moment the back door of the kitchen burst open and Pops rushed past us, holding, at arm's length, a flaming frying pan. He dropped it in the long grass, where it sizzled for a moment before the flame flickered and extinguished. Pops glared at the pan, then turned and went back into the kitchen.

'Fish balls,' he explained as he passed us.

I caught the puzzled look on Giles's face and burst out laughing.

I went to bed that night feeling that I'd never been this happy. I lay for ages, twisted into an uncomfortable position because Caliban had fallen asleep in the middle of my bed and was so deep into his wheezy snores that I didn't have the heart to shift him. I lay thinking about everything that had happened.

But I wasn't thinking straight. I didn't ask myself the question I should have asked as I drifted off to sleep with the sound of wind roaring like storm waves through the rowan trees. I didn't ask myself why, exactly, Imogen was so worried about me.

42

O n the day Mum was due to arrive the whole place was shrouded in mist. It even felt as though there was mist stealing under the front and back doors and down the hallway as Giles and I sat munching toast in the dining room.

I was trying to imagine what it would be like having Mum here, now it was finally going to happen. I wondered if the ground between us would have shifted and fractured. I wouldn't be able to tell until I saw her.

The town at which she'd be arriving on the monorail was a journey of about twenty kilometres beyond the village and we'd hired an electrocar. But I wasn't going with them to collect her because I wanted to stay and finish my final painting so that she could see them all—see what I'd been trying to do.

The other thing was that Pops wasn't too good that morning. When I'd taken him his tea he'd had a chesty cough that I didn't like the sound of and Becky agreed with me that he'd better see a doctor, just in case. She'd got him an appointment with the doctor in the village and they were all going off earlier than planned.

'How is he?' I asked as Becky came down. She'd found some cough medicine for him to take.

'Oh, he's quite cheerful in himself and it may be that the cough stuff will do the trick, but I think it's the right thing to do, to take him into the surgery. Don't want to take any chances.'

'Absolutely not. Thanks, Becky,' I said.

Giles licked the butter off his fingers and started collecting the plates.

'Now, are you sure you don't want to come with us?' he said.

'We can't fit everyone in the car,' I said.

'I know. So I can stay here,' said Becky.

'I want to stay, really.'

I could tell by the way she glanced at me that she suspected something was up with me. And there was. I don't know how much of it was that I wanted to get the painting right to show Mum and how much was just that I was nervous about seeing her again. Anyway, I wanted to stay. I wanted some time on my own.

'I'll be OK,' I said. 'And if Pops is happy to go without me, then I'm better off staying here, finishing the painting and getting everything ready for Mum.'

I took the plates from Giles and began washing them up. I looked out through the kitchen window. The pines behind the cottage were dark smudges in the mist and everything seemed to be dripping—drops falling from the guttering, the shining leaves of the evergreen bushes, the upturned wheelbarrow.

'We won't be all that long,' said Giles. 'We'll get some shopping too. Where's the list?'

'Hall table,' said Becky.

'Can you add chocolate doughnuts?' I called down the hall after him.

'Consider it done. Sure you'll be OK?'

'Of course. Off you go.'

Quarter of an hour later I tucked Pops snugly into the front of the electrocar and waved as it crunched down the driveway and out of sight behind the laurel bushes. I heard the whine of it picking up speed in the lane and then it was gone. I turned back to the cottage, which sat silently on its wet lawn, the mist from the lake draped around it. I

228

was glad to have the place to myself for the morning. I had a lot to do.

I went back into the study, where the painting was set up ready for work. I slumped down onto the musty sofa, staring into the picture, dreaming my way into it, trying to find why it had never quite worked. And suddenly I knew what I had to do. I jumped up, put the painting aside and took a new sheet of paper. Begin again. It was the only way.

It must have been an hour or so later, when I was deep into the new painting, that I became conscious of a tiny noise. A plaintive, smothered ringing. I looked up from my work, seeing immediately that the mist outside had thickened, was pressing close against the window. I listened. The sound was far too faint to be the landline phone. I stood up, went to the door and opened it. The noise was closer now, and I realized that it was a mobile. Giles must have left it behind. He was the only one who had a mobile.

I followed the sound down the hall to Giles's battered old leather coat, the bleating from the pocket getting louder all the time. I fished around amongst wrappers, hankies, a bit of string, and finally dredged up the mobile. I pressed the green bar.

'Hello?'

'Giles?' A woman's voice. Urgent.

I hesitated a second. 'It's Dominic,' I said.

'Dominic! Are you in the cottage?'

'Who is this?'

'It's Imogen. If you're in the cottage, I want you to get out. Now.'

'What?'

'Where are you? I need to know where you are!' She sounded frantic now.

'Yes, I'm in Giles and Becky's cottage, but how . . . ?'

'You're not safe there, Dominic. Trust me. Do you know the fishing hut in the next valley?'

229

My mind was churning. The impossibility of this. How did Imogen know anything about cottages and valleys . . . I mentally scanned the landscape I knew so well and suddenly I saw the stone hut in the lonely valley, its roof mossed and sagging . . . 'Yes!' I cried. 'I know where you mean!'

'Get out of the cottage immediately and go to the hut. I'll come and meet you.'

'Why?'

'The place isn't safe for you any more. Just get yourself to the hut. Trust me.'

'Why? Why should I trust you?'

A crackling sound chopped her voice into pieces. I thought I'd made out the last bit.

'Above me?' I yelled into the tiny phone, my voice echoing off the flagstoned floor. 'What's above me?'

'I said . . . because I . . . ' And now it sounded as if her voice was being buffeted by the wind. Finally, it cut out altogether.

'Imogen . . . ?'

But the line was dead. I pressed the code to see if I could get her back, but there was just a series of bleeps and I didn't know what that meant.

I stood for long seconds, the silence in the hallway deepening. There was no sound, not even the breathing of the lake out there in the fog. I could almost hear my heartbeat. What the hell was she doing in Scotland? And why on earth should I trust her, after last time? Why couldn't she just leave me alone?

And then I realized. She would have left me alone if she could. But something must have happened. And now I had to do as she said, I had to get out. I was her death sentence. Which meant that she wouldn't risk being anywhere near me unless there was a reason. A desperate reason.

I grabbed my coat, ran down the hall and out into the fog.

I headed for the dark smudges that marked the edge of the pine woods and darted in amongst the glistening black trunks. A few paces in I stopped, trying to calm my gasping breath as I watched and listened. The only sound came from the dripping of the trees.

I turned back into the woods, saw the long columns of identical straight trunks disappearing into the strange, thick-scented twilight, locked in by the feathered branches overhead.

I headed up the path as fast as I could, deeper and deeper into the trees. I dared not turn round. Because now a fear, a nightmare imagining, was gripping my mind. It was that the trees were closing in behind me, pressing closer and closer, pushing me, chasing me onwards. If I turned round they'd get me.

I ran on and on until, just before I reached the edge of the woods, I heard—and felt—a noise behind me. A thick, thudding sound as if something had fallen. And whatever it was, it was very close.

43

I darted behind a tree on the very edge of the woods, thick fog masking everything ahead of me. But behind me I could see, back into the trees.

There was someone on the ground, struggling to free her foot from the mossy web of a tree root. She gave the root a final, angry kick and picked herself up off the deep litter of pine needles. She stood, brushed herself down, swept the blonde hair from her face and looked around. I eased back behind my tree, heart thudding, trying to quieten my breathing. It was Leanne Kelsey and there could be only one reason for her being here.

I held my breath and waited, straining to hear the slightest sound. The sound of her smart hiking boots on the hollow, springy ground. The sound of twigs snapping. But there was nothing. Only thick, close silence.

And then she called out.

'Dominic Gordon! Oh, Do-mi-nic! Don't make me chase you any more, sweetie! I can tramp through these woods for as long as I have to, but there is an easier way, you know!'

I heard the crump of her boots nearby. She walked into my line of vision, up towards the edge of the wood. I froze. If she turned round now, she would see me, but I dared not move in case I made her turn. As slowly as I could, millimetre by millimetre, I pulled back. She flicked her hair back, seemed to listen for a moment. Then she clenched her fists and cried out, 'Damn!'

She turned away and stomped back down the path.

I leaned against the tree. Waited. When I thought I'd waited long enough, I slowly eased my head round, took a look.

The lines of trees stretched back, deep into the darkness. Nothing moving. No sound. I watched a few moments more and then stepped out from behind my tree.

And she was on me so fast that I screamed out in terror, not knowing what hit me first: the triumphant yell of 'Gotcha!', the sickly perfume, her arms pushing me back against the tree. She stood in front of me, grinning. She scraped a hand through her glossy hair and blew out a sigh.

'You're a tough one to catch,' she said. 'But you shouldn't believe all that stuff about journalists being chain-smoking alcoholics. I'm as fit as a flea, as you can see. You do know who I am, don't you?'

'I'm afraid not.' I tried to keep my voice steady, tried to match her gaze strength for strength.

She held out a hand for me to shake. 'My name is Leanne. As I say, I'm a journalist. Oh, but maybe Rebecca will have told you. Like Rebecca, I'm an old friend of your brother's.' She dropped her hand and gave another smirking smile. 'And I'm the only one who knows the truth about you—who you are and how you came to be.'

'Look, I'm sorry, I don't know who you think I am . . .' I said.

'I've just told you, I *know* who you are. We need to talk about how we're going to play this,' she said. 'If you make the right decisions now, you're going to be a very rich man indeed.'

Everything inside me was roaring and racing, the blood hurtling round my body, making me shake. I knew she could see it. And a voice in my head was screaming, run, run!

'It's interesting, isn't it?' she said. 'Nick was a brilliant scientist and you—well, with a little training, I think we could market you as the artistic genius. Two sides of the same coin. What do you say, Dominic?'

She reached inside her jacket and produced a small sketchbook. One of mine. I recognized it immediately. I'd lost it, or thought I had, down by the lake the day before.

She took off her gloves and flicked through the book, her perfect red nails digging into the paper. I was beginning to feel a pool of calm within the rush of anger and fear. I didn't know how I was going to fight her, but she wasn't going to get me without a fight. I watched her turn the pages of my book and waited until my breathing had calmed.

'I don't know what you're talking about,' I said, 'but that book is my property.'

'*My* property, sweetheart. I think you'll find that everything about you is my property now. You'll also find that it will pay you to be nice to me. Perhaps you didn't understand me when I said I'm a journalist. I have access to the top editors and programmers all around the world. That makes me a dangerous person to have as an enemy.'

She leaned in close. I backed up, stumbled against the tree. I could feel her breath puffing onto my face as she spoke.

'Let's just recap, in case Rebecca didn't show you my emails. The story begins on the Cayman Islands, March 2001. One fine morning, the brilliant Professor Holt arrives at a research station that happens to be owned by a subsidiary of Gordon's Pharmaceuticals. Not far away, at an exclusive hotel, Mr and Mrs Michael Gordon book in . . . ' She paused and her grey eyes raked all over me. 'And nine months later, their dead son is made to breathe again.'

'I'm NOT Nick! You don't understand.'

'No, *you* don't understand, Mr head-in-the-clouds artist! This story is bursting to come out. If it comes out through me, I can make sure you get what you want out of it. I print the stories, which means that you can print your own money. Believe me, you're not going to get a better deal. I know what they're like, some of the people in my profession, once they get hold of a story. Play it my way and if ever you want out, well—there are ways and means of buying a new identity.'

'Why would I want a new identity?' I said calmly. 'I like the one I have.'

Suddenly she slipped a hand under my jacket, tugged at my jumper and shirt. I felt her icy hand against the small of my back.

'*God*, you are like your brother, aren't you? Stubborn as hell! Let's see just *how* like him! Let's have a look at that birthmark.'

'Get OFF me!' I yelled.

But she hooked her leg around mine, kicked it out from under me so that we both fell onto the mattress of needles. She rolled on top of me.

'It took me a while to suss it,' she grinned. 'Silly old me. Should have boned up on the cloning process—what it means. And what it means is—your mother gave birth to the same baby twice.'

'That's rubbish!' I yelled.

She smirked and continued, 'Which means that both babies would have been born with this rather dramatic birthmark.'

Her hands were working my shirt loose at the front, pulling it upwards. She was laughing, her breath puffing onto my face. Every single bit of me was tingling with revulsion. I pushed her with all my strength.

'Get OFF!'

I heard my own yell muffle into the trees as I threw her off me and scrambled to my feet. I ran out of the woods. I ran blind until I heard the river churning over the rocks ahead. I stumbled and scrambled on all fours up the steep path by the water's edge, the cold fog ripping into my lungs.

It was my only hope, to go up into the high mountains. I could make it through the fog, I just had to concentrate on the path, remember the rocks, the cairns, all the little landmarks that I knew so well.

Let her follow if she dared, she wouldn't catch me. I could move fast. And I knew where I was going.

44

That's how it happened that I headed for the last time towards my vantage point on the summit of the ridge. It was the only place left to go. As I'd climbed higher the fog had thinned and by the time I reached the top and picked my way across the knife-edge to the safety of the rocks, there was just low cloud scudding and swirling around me.

I huddled back into the familiar hollow of my rocky outcrop and closed my eyes, listening to the mountain catch the wind and make music of it. I hadn't come all this way just to be someone else's property, someone else's puppet instead of my father's. I had to find a way to fight her.

I'd not been there long when I heard a scrabbling sound and the clack, clack of falling rock. I snapped my eyes open to see, just beyond the flat rock at the other end of the ridge, a blonde head appear. Then the rest of her. I couldn't believe she'd followed me.

Leanne Kelsey stood on the slab of rock, panting to get her breath back, looking across at me with a smile. 'Game over, Dominic,' she said. 'What a wonderful hiding place!'

I leaned back against the rock, smiling to myself. Of course she knew my hiding place. Everything was becoming perfectly clear now. She must have been watching for weeks, waiting to make her move. The fishing boat that I kept seeing down on the lake . . . it would be the perfect observation point. She'd been watching me. If only I'd figured that out sooner, I wouldn't have come up here. I stared across at her smug grin. I mustn't let it wind me up.

'The thing is,' I said, 'if you've been hanging round here watching me all this time and you reckon you've got this mind-blowing story to tell about me—why haven't you made your move before?'

'Haven't been hanging round here long. Only arrived yesterday, as it happens.'

I watched her as she sat down, cross-legged, on the flat slab of rock and lit a cigarette. The smoke drifted with the veils of cloud that were shifting behind her. OK, so I'd been wrong about her watching. But even so, she could have made her move sooner.

'You haven't a shred of real proof that what you say is true, have you?' I said.

She ignored this, puffed out smoke and asked, 'So how did you get to know them? Giles and Becky.'

'My parents kept in touch with them after Nick died,' I said.

'Must have been tough growing up in the shadow of such a genius,' she said. 'They did tell you about him, didn't they?'

'Yes, of course.'

'When did you first meet Imogen?'

'Imogen who?' I said.

'Professor Imogen Holt, your creator.'

'She's not my creator and I've never met her,' I said, careful of my voice.

'You've never been to her house?'

'I've just said, I don't know her.'

'You've never been to her house?'

'No.'

'You painted rather a good picture of it, though, didn't you?'

I felt my face redden. So she'd got into Imogen's home too. Must keep cool. 'No, I've never been there,' I said.

'Poor old Imogen. She must be in a real panic,'

continued Leanne. 'I paid her the courtesy of letting her know that I've discovered the truth, of course. But she's going to have a job tracking you down. I let it be known that you'd been whisked off to the States. So no doubt she'll have gone rushing across the Atlantic to look for her baby. Naughty little me.'

She took another drag of her cigarette.

'You know she only did it because Nick was such a genius, don't you?' she said. 'That's why they all wanted him back. Mr Bloody Perfect. God, what a fuss when he died! Giles devastated, Rebecca bleating like a lost lamb. What's it like to have a second-hand life? That's what people are going to want to know. Quite an interesting concept, really.'

'You were so jealous of Becky, weren't you?' I said. 'Sounds like you still are.'

'Jealous of *her*? Do me a favour!'

'OK, I'll do you a favour.' I stood up. 'If you want the truth, I'll tell you the truth. Becky's worth ten of you, and so is Giles. They were good friends to Nick. They loved him and he loved them. And for some reason you can't forgive him for loving them and not you. So you think you've found a way to pay everyone back. Well, you're not going to get what you want, Leanne. However much you hound me, you're not going to get what you *really* want!'

She stared across at me, then chucked her cigarette over the edge of the slab, down into the cloud. She dragged something out of the pocket of her jacket and held it up for me to see. Her mobile, of course.

'I'm bored with the game now, Dominic. The world has a right to know this story. I press one button and everything I know flies to the major newsdesks all round the world. It's a shame to do it this way, but if you don't want to deal with me I'll have to unleash the real bloodhounds. The media heavyweights. They'll crack you open like an egg, sweetheart!'

'There's no need,' I said. 'I've decided what I'm going to do.'

'Oh, really? You think you've got a choice any more? This I've got to hear!'

A gust of wind surged up the sheer slope below us, pushing at the cloud behind the slab on which Leanne sat. There was only a thin veil now and I saw, or thought I saw, a shadow moving behind it, moving closer to Leanne. The wind gusted again, hiding the shadow for a few seconds and then the cloud cleared completely and I saw who it was. She raised an arm to pull the hood from her head, to show tendrils of blonde hair blowing across her face. My heart hammered. No, no, no! Not Imogen! She mustn't be here now! Go back, go back!

As Leanne moved to put her mobile away, Imogen sprang forward and took a swipe at the hand that held it. Leanne twisted round and cried out in shock. Then she began to laugh.

'Good God, I don't believe it! The proof! The proof here in person! Jeez, I wish I'd brought the film crew!'

Imogen grabbed again for the mobile and missed. Leanne twisted further round and got hold of Imogen's leg. But now she had shifted her weight closer to the edge of the slab, to where it tilted sharply down towards the drop. Imogen fell forwards as her leg was pulled from under her, and Leanne, not realizing what was happening in time to let go, was dragged with her.

They both fell. Disappeared over the edge so quickly they didn't even scream. I saw the slight movement of cloud as they were swallowed up. I scrambled out of my hollow and down onto the ridge. I looked over.

One of them had managed to cling on to the narrow

ledge below the ridge. I saw a bloodied forearm, a flash of blonde hair. She looked up at me.

'Imogen! Hang on, I can get to you!' I cried.

'NO! Stay where you are!'

I lowered myself to a sitting position on the ridge.

'DON'T!' she said.

Part of the ledge gave way and she struggled to cling on to what was left. The sound of falling rock echoed off the mountain walls. Clack . . . clack. I lowered myself onto the scree. It started to slide. It was no good. I'd just be sending rock down on top of her. I pulled myself back onto the ridge and called down to her, 'I'm coming down onto the ledge. I know how to get there.'

'Stay there!'

'No! Just hold on! I can reach you!' I called. 'Everything's going to be all right!'

'Dominic, promise me! Always remember . . . '

It all happened at the same time. I was almost onto the ledge when I looked down and saw her face. She never finished what she was going to say because she fell. She fell into the clouds. I closed my eyes, and clung to the cold rock as the dizziness swept over me. It felt as if the mountain was moving, sending the pit of my stomach into sickening free-fall, falling with her.

I don't know how long it was that I clung there. I don't know how long before the sound of shattering rockfall stopped echoing off the mountain walls.

I am high up in the mountains, sitting on their shoulders, breathing the rock-cold smell of sheep and earth and granite. Way down below me, where the dark slopes plunge towards each other, a pale mass is floating in the valley. A whipped-cream of mist. The sun is bleeding over the ridge opposite, but it hasn't got down into the valley yet. Somewhere down in that valley there are dead bodies. Dead because of me.

A crow squarks, sudden and close. It is time to begin the journey home.

45

Now the mist has lifted completely and I'm sitting on my boulder by the lake. Mum and Becky and Giles are in the cottage, talking about what I've told them. After Giles and Becky had taken Pops to the doctor and picked up Mum from the monorail, they'd stopped off in the village to buy a few things. The woman in the newsagent had told them there'd been a blonde lady asking questions about us. Apparently she'd first been spotted yesterday and one of the customers reckoned they'd seen her somewhere before, but couldn't remember where.

So they'd rushed back here and begun the search. At last Giles had found me coming down off the mountain.

I'd said I wanted to be by myself for a while but now I can hear them coming. Giles comes to stand beside me.

'We'll have to tell the police something,' he says gently. 'But we need to decide exactly what we're going to say and stick to it. Becky thinks there's a way of explaining things without . . . well, we don't need to tell them the truth about you.'

'We do,' I say.

A second of silence, then Mum says, 'Are you sure? Dominic, you know what that means.'

I can hear the tears in her voice.

'We need to tell the truth,' I say. 'There's no good reason for doing what Dad and Imogen did. You can recreate a face, flesh and blood and bone. But what do those things matter? What have they ever mattered? A life can't be replaced. And babies aren't products, they shouldn't be made-to-order commodities forced to live to some sort of template, someone else's idea of perfection. Becky, I need your help.'

Becky swipes her sleeve across her eyes, 'You've got it.'

'I'm going to tell my story, but it's got to be told in *my* way, to people who will listen. You know some people—journalists—don't you?'

She nods and holds my gaze and I know she believes I can do it.

I stay here on my boulder while they go and call the police. I'm listening to the gentle breathing of the lake and painting a picture of Imogen in my head. I'll never know for certain if she let go on purpose. But she knew she could never pull herself up without help. And I might not have been able to hold her.

Had it been her in that rowing boat all along, watching over me? Maybe, maybe not. But if it had been her, she'd been taking a terrible risk. Why hadn't she just run, like my father had? And what did she want me to remember?

I think I know part of it. Mum had given me the clue, all those weeks ago when she'd said that Imogen would never let anyone hurt me. I was her child, in a way.

Whatever it was that she wanted me to remember, I'll never know for certain. So I'll decide for myself what I want to remember. I'll remember that no matter how bad things get, I'd rather be me than anyone else. I'll remember those honey-hazel eyes, those lioness eyes that last looked up at me from a mass of sharp, sliding rock. I'll remember Pops and his bald old head full of forgotten memories, and Mum with her leaky emotions and passionate heart, and Giles and Becky. And Nick.

All unique and unrepeatable, like cloud-shadows on mountains or flames in a fire.

Other Oxford fiction

Starseeker
Tim Bowler
ISBN 0 19 275305 3

Luke is in trouble. Skin and the gang have a job for him.
They want him to break into Mrs Little's house and steal
the jewellery box. They want him to prove that he's got
what it takes. That he's part of the gang.

But Luke finds more than just a jewellery box in the
house. He finds something so unexpected it will change
his life forever . . .

'Don't miss it.'
Melvin Burgess

'A fantastic book.'
Sunday Express

Calling a Dead Man
Gillian Cross
ISBN 0 19 275190 5

How did John Cox die? His sister Hayley thinks she
knows, but she wants to see the place where it happened.
With John's friend Annie she travels to Russia to visit the
site of the explosion that killed him. But they soon realize
that there is more to John's death than meets the eye. And
certain people are desperate to keep them from finding out
the truth.

Meanwhile, deep in the wastes of Siberia, a man with no
memory and a high fever stumbles out of the forest . . .

'extraordinary and ambitious . . . this convincing, dark
story is one of the author's best'

The Independent

Going For Stone
Philip Gross
ISBN 0 19 275308 8

Nick is desperate—out on the streets, in a strange town, with no money, no ID.

He's got nothing to lose.

Then he meets Swan and the others. Human statues. Street performers who can turn themselves to stone—almost. Could he do that?

He finds he's good at it. Very good.

Soon he and Swan are working with the mysterious Antonin, tucked away in his secret academy. There they will learn to be more like stone than ever.

But perhaps it's possible to go too far in going for stone. Perhaps the high walls of Antonin's academy hide more danger than Nick and Swan could ever have imagined . . .

'Wonderfully scary and unusual'
Adele Geras, The Guardian

'Haunting and unforgettable'
Independent on Sunday

Follow Me Down
Julie Hearn
ISBN 0 19 271927 0

Something odd is going on in the basement of an old
house in east London. Tom, visiting his gran, finds the
gap forming. And the voices are calling him . . .

Tom takes a leap into the early eighteenth century—to a
time when 'monsters' like the Bendy Man and the Gorilla
Woman appeared at Bartholomew Fair . . . a time when
doctors paid a high price for unusual bodies to experiment
on—and 'monsters' were prime targets.

Can Tom save the Giant? Will he and his friends rescue
him from a fate worse than death? It is a desperate race
against time. Meanwhile, Tom has problems of his own to
contend with. Illness. Family secrets. A rift between his
mum and his gran.

In the present, as well as the past, Tom must learn to look
beyond appearances.

'someone whose work I always read with pleasure'
Philip Pullman

'*Follow Me Down* leaps so many gaps—between present and
past, good and evil, life and death, the ordinary and the
truly extraordinary.'
Geraldine McCaughrean